Pioneer Legacy

Norene Morris

A sequel to *Rainbow Harvest*.

Heartsong Presents

Dedication

"To Jean, my Dear Friend,
Christian Sister and Patient Listener."

A note from the Author:
*I love to hear from my readers! You may write to me at the
following address:*

Norene Morris
Author Relations
P.O. Box 719
Uhrichsville, OH 44683

ISBN 1-55748-614-X

PIONEER LEGACY

Tom veered the wagon into a cluster of Siberian elm trees for relief and protection from the hot June sun. Tommy and Beth had been a cranky handful for Mary Lou the last hour, and a rear wagon wheel had begun to wiggle precariously a couple miles back.

Tom jumped from the wagon, patted each horse's face as he rounded the front of the team, stretched his arms for a twin, swung them to the ground, then reached for Mary Lou.

Mary Lou leaned her waist into Tom's hands and jumped. The ground felt restfully solid after their jostling ride all morning. Gratefully accepting the welcome shade, she slid her bonnet off her head and tousled her hair, relishing even a hot breeze through it.

Tom continued to the wheel, ran his hands over it and stooped to inspect it. "Looks like I'm going to have to tighten this wheel before we go on. That will delay us a bit. Too bad it could not have held out till we got to the river. Now, we will barely make Red River Station by suppertime and will have to wait until morning to cross over into the Nations."

"The Nations? Where is that?" Mary Lou had heard of it but never really knew where it was.

"It's Indian Territory on the other side of the Red River. Texas laws don't apply. We may meet a few Indians."

Mary Lou knew Kansas Indians but—

"Don't worry, I know sign language, and Mother gave me some cloth, beads and feathers to give them if we get stopped. They don't bother people like they used to. I remember one cattle drive with Father and Smitty. An Indian rode into camp with one finger raised demanding a dollar a head to cross over his tribal lands. Father refused to pay it. The Indians stampeded the herd, cut off six cows and drove them off. I was only fourteen, but I remember that we had one wild time gaining control of that herd."

Sharp fingers of fear scratched at Mary Lou's stomach. She didn't remember being afraid when she and Tom made the trip to Texas from Kansas. All she could recall was the overwhelming love she felt for her new husband and the consuming thoughts of meeting Tom's family. This time was different—the twins. . . . She shook her head to dispel a disturbing uneasiness. She needed to get busy. "Will I have time to make something to eat?"

Tom nodded and grinned. "Ma'am, my stomach sure would appreciate it." His admiring eyes danced love across the space between them. Suddenly, he rose from the wheel and his feet followed his gaze. Tom took Mary Lou into his arms and captured her lips for a long, sweet kiss. "Been wanting to do that all morning," he said in her ear and hugged her close.

Mary Lou relaxed in his embrace, her body tiredness eased. Tom's arms always had a soothing effect. Her arms pressed him closer while her heart pounded its thanks to God for His gift of a good, loving husband. Suddenly an unnatural quietness invaded the loving moment and struck fear into her heart. "The twins. . . ."

They turned in time to see Beth disappearing into the

high grass that surrounded them. Mary Lou hurried to pick her up. Tom checked the drag marks on the dusty ground and followed them into grass higher than his knees.

Her heart pounding, Mary Lou watched Tom search the tall grass. He walked slowly, parting the grass with his left hand, the right poised at his holster.

"Tommy. Where are you, son? Come to papa," he called softly.

Suddenly, Tom whisked his pistol from its holster and shot into the grass.

Tommy screamed.

Mary Lou's mind exploded with the shot! Tom shot— "Tommy," she screamed. Her stunned body refused to move.

Tom bent into the grass and raised up with Tommy in his arms.

"Oh, Tom," she screamed, tears of relief flooded her cheeks. "Why did you shoot?"

Tom poked his gun back into the grass and came up with a dead rattlesnake draped over it. "I had to shoot. This fellow was curling up for business. If Tommy had moved or I would have reached for him, the snake would have struck."

Mary Lou threw herself and Beth against her husband and son. Tom's free arm wound around her in comfort. Tommy squirmed in the tight embrace and hollered.

Tom and Mary Lou discovered they had to keep a closer eye on their little son who was delighted with his new mobility. His crawl on one knee and one leg sped him across a floor or ground as fast as Mary Lou could walk. Any little movement sparked Tommy's curiosity and lured him off to investigate. One day he picked up a bee, put it in his mouth, made a wry face, and quickly spit out the startled insect before it had a chance to use its weapon.

Beth, enthralled and fascinated by her brother's busyness, followed him everywhere and did everything he did.

Tom plopped Tommy beside him on the ground, and he watched with avid interest as his father built a fire. Tom carried the boy to sit beside him while he worked on the wheel and kept him immobile by handing him tools. Tom ruffled Tommy's hair and grinned as he retrieved a wrench from his son. "Gotta make a rancher out of you, young-un, and this is where you start—learning how to fix things."

Beth crawled over and sat with the men.

Mary Lou cooked and fed each twin mash with egg, then nursed them to settle them down. They hadn't slept much during the morning. Hopefully, they would bed down for a nap in the kiddie coop Tom had made behind the front seat of the wagon and give everybody a rest.

Tom paused in his repairs long enough to eat beef jerky, a couple pieces of Hattie's homemade bread, and a delicious apple hand pie.

Tucked at the bottom of Hattie's basket, Mary Lou found biscuits, smoked ham, and a large jar of canned peaches. Bless her, she thought to herself. Mary Lou repacked the basket and put it near the back of the wagon where she could easily retrieve it for supper.

Tom checked the other wheels. "Good as new," he said, climbed aboard, and handed Mary Lou up into the wagon seat beside him. "Glad we are heading north. Won't have to face that sun."

Nevertheless, a hot afternoon dragged on. Fortunately, the wagon rolled in and around the ruts of the trail and rocked the twins to sleep.

Mary Lou asked, "Any idea how long it will take us to get home?"

"We can only go about four to five miles an hour. Probably a good week to get to Venture after we cross the river. We should reach Red River Station before suppertime, sleep on this side and cross over in the morning. That way, the wagon will be dry to bed down tonight, and we will be able to dry out as we travel tomorrow."

Tom sensed Mary Lou's uneasiness about crossing. He reached over and patted her hand. "The water will be a little high at this time of the year because of the swell of spring rains, but there will be plenty of help from the cowboys at the station to get us across safely." He glanced at his wife and grinned. "So don't worry, little Mama."

She returned a half-brave smile. It amazed her how often Tom read her mind. She watched her strong, confident husband seated beside her, feet braced, reins loose, but firm in his hands.

In their nearly two years as man and wife, Tom had more than displayed his ability to handle every situation they had faced and proved that his uppermost thought was always for his family, not only she and the twins, but his mother, his brothers, and even the housekeeper Hattie, who treated him like the son she had lost.

Big Jon Wimbley rose in Mary Lou's mind; he was a giant of a man in soul as well as in stature and was her measure of a true family man. In her growing years, after Pa's accident, he gathered her in with his own twelve and became her substitute father. When Mama died, Big Jon gave her the comfort and consolation her own father, in his grief, denied her. Mary Lou's conscience twinged. It was unfair to measure Pa against Big Jon. She felt like a traitor,

yet looked forward to seeing Big Jon more than she did her
father.

Weeks before they began their trip to Kansas, the hurt-
ful question nagged. What kind of a reception would Pa
give her when they arrived? She had written faithfully
every month, but had never received an answer. The only
letters she received were from Aunt Nelda, Aunt Tibby,
and Jenny. Not even a small note from Pa at Christmastime
about the socks she had knitted for him. Aunt Nelda wrote
that since he had given the back rooms of the store to Glenn,
Pa seemed glad to come home most nights. Mary Lou
prayed that her time away had softened his anger so they
could talk and that he had forgiven her for marrying a cowboy. Hopefully, he had learned the truth that she had not
neglected Mama.

Mama. In Mary Lou's reasoning mind, two years should
have eased the ache of Mama's death but her heart told her
it hadn't. In times alone, even surrounded with the joy and
abundance of her life with Tom, his family, and the twins,
she longingly envisioned Mama sitting in her rocker with
Tommy and Beth in her arms, her face beaming with pride
and joy as she cradled her grandbabies. The vision never
failed to provoke a spontaneous rush of tears. If possible,
she missed Mama even more. She needed Mama to teach
her how she gleaned such strengthening wisdom from the
Bible for every situation and how to be a good mother.
Slowly, Mary Lou made discoveries of her own with the
help of underlined passages and word meanings written in
the margins in Mama's precise schoolteacher script. They
called Mary Lou's attention to a gem she probably would
have missed. Mama's Bible lay safely tucked in her carpet bag with her clothes. She would get it out in the

morning, and perhaps when the twins napped, she would read aloud to Tom; and they would mull over God's encouraging words as they traveled.

The rhythmic clip, clop of the horses hooves hitting the hard trail accelerated Mary Lou's excitement at the thought of seeing her two aunts. She could envision them when they saw the twins. They would be ecstatic!

Suddenly, in the distance, a swishing sound rose and grew louder as they travelled.

Tom looked at Mary Lou and grinned. "Well, it won't be long now. That's the Red River you hear."

Mary Lou squelched a rising apprehension and watched a small speck on the horizon grow into a rough border town squatted on the approaching shore. Streamside trees held grotesque tangles of driftwood in their branches betraying the magnitude of past floods. A short distance from the shore at one side of the buildings was a rude cemetery of bizarre crosses leaning haphazardly over graves of men who had been killed or drowned during cattle crossings.

Tom pulled the team to a halt. "Red River Station," he called and perused the river. "Oh, that's not bad. We'll float across easily. I even think the wheels might touch." Float across! In a loaded wagon? Mary Lou lifted her eyes. *I need lots more faith, Lord!*

Two cowboys appeared from the side of a building.

"Tom!" one of them hollered, yanked off his hat and waved it vigorously over his head. "You goin' over now or waitin' 'til morning'"

Tom waved back. "Ho, Lannie! We'll cross tomorrow. You and Shade going to be here in the morning?"

"Yep, we'll be here." The cowboys followed the wagon

as Tom pulled it off to the side of the buildings. When the wagon stopped, the twins woke and clamored to get out of the kiddie coop.

Lannie's eyebrows raised. "Well, whatdaya know! These here your young-uns?"

"Yep," Tom said with noticeable pride as he climbed into the back and handed Beth down to Lannie. She was not quite sure she wanted to leave her papa.

Lannie took her and held her high in the air. "Well, I'll be," he said, "She's gonna be as purty as her ma one of these days."

It was Mary Lou's turn to swell with pride.

Tom filled Shade's outstretched arms with a wary Tommy who squinted dubious brows at his receiver.

Shade laughed. "This boy's a real bruiser. He'll make some kind of tough cowboy when he hits thirteen."

Mary Lou marveled that Lennie and Shade seemed so at home with her babies but she could not quite picture Tommy as a cowboy, yet.

"I'm hoping he will make a great rancher like his grand-father," Tom said.

Or like his father, Mary Lou thought. Her heart swelled, and she prayed that Tommy would not only look like, but act like Tom. Tommy's present escapades sometimes planted small seeds of doubt. But then, she hadn't known Tom as a little boy. She smiled. She had a hunch he had been as rambunctious as his busy, little son.

Finally, Lannie and Shade handed the twins back to their parents. Mary Lou noticed several rain barrels along the side of the main building. The two with dippers hung on nails above were obviously for drinking. The other three spaced separately were for washing. Tom held the twins while Mary Lou washed the surface grime from their hands and faces and dried them on her apron. Tantalizing smells wafted beneath her nose. Suddenly, Mary Lou was ravenous.

Inside, the building was dim. The walls were wallpapered with newsprint, put there mainly for warmth, but still readable where it was not covered with maps, a post card here and there, cattle breeding charts, various photographs, old calendar pictures and even demure pinups.

Tom seated Mary Lou at a table. Immediately, a stocky woman, accompanied by smells from the kitchen, emerged with long, well-used strips of cloth to tie Beth and Tommy into their chairs. Mary Lou smiled. "Thank you. They are used to that. Until their father made high chairs for Christmas, we did exactly what you are doing."

The woman's merry eyes spoke her welcome. She clucked both babies' chins. "Don't get many wee ones here. 'Tis a pleasure to see them. They twins?"

Mary Lou nodded and smiled again. The woman's voice was soft, lilting and almost gentle, a surprise coming from someone who must have spent most of her life around boisterous cowboys and cattlemen. "Yes, this is Beth, and this is Tommy."

The twins stared wide-eyed as the woman moved around their chairs and tied them in. She patted the top of Tommy's head and smoothed her hand over Beth's curls, then returned to stand beside Mary Lou. "We have beef, pork, fried potatoes, sourdough biscuits, cowboy beans, and vinegar pie."

Tom ordered some of each, Mary Lou took beef, sourdough biscuits, a piece of vinegar pie, and an order of mashed cowboy beans for the twins.

As they ate, cowboys stopped at the table for a few words with Tom. They were a jolly, sociable bunch of surprisingly young men. It wasn't easy to tell their ages. Yet, Mary Lou guessed which ones were twelve to fourteen. They were boisterous and strutted around pretending to be older.

When Tom finished eating, he told Mary Lou he wanted to talk to Lannie and Shade about plans to cross the river in the morning. He picked up his tin cup of coffee and joined them.

Mary Lou finished feeding the twins, glancing at Tom now and then. She could tell from their motions that he and the boys were discussing details of the crossing. Then, they laughingly began to josh Tom. From a word she heard now and then and through their motions, Mary Lou surmised they wanted Tom to come back to the station with them after he settled his family. Tom shook his head, rose and returned to Mary Lou.

Tom moved the wagon away from the buildings under a tree for privacy. Tired, cranky twins finally settled in the kiddie coop for the night. Mary Lou and Tom snuggled together in blankets under the wagon and listened to the cowboys songs and laughter from the big building at the far end.

"Would you rather be over in the other building having a good time with the cowboys or—" She never finished her sentence. Tom's mouth closed over hers. Talking ceased.

two

Tom slowly slipped from their blanket bed under the wagon, stood up, stretched, appraised the day, and climbed into dew-damp clothes.

It was early. The sun, its eye only half open, had not emanated enough heat to dispel the sleepy morning mist that blinked and sparkled on blades of prairie grass in answer to the sun's wake-up call. Even the brown river water flowed drowsily, soothed by a calm night.

Good, Tom thought, it will make crossing the river easier for everyone. As he rounded the other side of the wagon, he paused, stood and gazed at his beautiful, sleeping wife. Long, chestnut waves spilled casually around her shoulders. He loved to touch those soft, silky strands and watch her braid and unbraid her hair. He knelt on one knee beside her and pushed stray locks from her pug nose. He loved that, too. When she laughed, it wiggled bunny fashion.

"Papa, papa," came a call from the wagon.

Tom grinned. Mary Lou always spoke to the children about their "papa," and Tommy within the last week discovered the word connected him with his father. The call tugged at Tom's heart. He reached into the wagon and lifted his son from the kiddie coup. Beth sat rubbing her eyes, then stretched her arms forward. He deposited them one by one on the ground, and they crawled to their mother under the wagon. Tom went to feed and water Buttermilk and Babe.

Their call woke Mary Lou, then she felt them as they nuzzled her. She sat up amazed. She had not felt Tom slip from her side. He had decided last night they would have breakfast in the station so she wouldn't have to pack and unpack to prepare a morning meal. Her body evidently seized the opportunity to rest, its first chance to release itself from all the preparations and work of the trip. She rose, dressed quickly, and nursed the twins. Tom draped their bedding over the seat of the wagon, hoping the sun would dry out some of the night's dampness. On their way to breakfast, they paused to splash water on their hands and faces before they went into the station.

"Good morning," welcomed the same cheery woman from last night. She tied the twins in their chairs, and patted their heads.

The menu was much the same as supper the night before, flapjacks, steak and fried potatoes, but thick, steamy oatmeal was added to the breakfast menu. The parents shared their oatmeal with the twins.

Mary Lou sensed an urgency in Tom. They ate quickly and hurried back to the wagon to get ready to cross the river.

Only the twins were content with the moment. They sat on the ground playing with stones. Tommy popped one in his mouth then spit it out. Beth, watching him, did the same, made a face, opened her mouth, and it rolled off her tongue to the ground.

Tom hitched the team and moved the wagon to the edge of the river. On the other side, Lannie, Shade, and three cowboys on horseback appeared and waved.

Mary Lou picked up the twins and followed the wagon. Tom helped her into the seat and knotted a long rope around her waist. He took a shorter rope, looped it through the one tied around Mary Lou's middle, then tied a twin at each end so they were tied to their mother.

Tommy squalled and squirmed to get loose.

"Be still, son!" Tom's stern tone caught Tommy's attention. Two pairs of intensely blue eyes met and challenged. The boy's squalling quieted, his pet lip receded, and he stuck his thumb in his mouth, his gaze still anchored on his father. A second later he pulled out his thumb and his face exploded into a wide grin that squiggled his tiny nose. Tom stroked Tommy's chin, patted the top of his head, and smiled. "Be a good little man, son. We have to take care of our women." He gathered the rope connected to the twins and looked seriously into Mary Lou's eyes. "Hang on to both of these with one hand and the wagon with the other." Tom turned, hollered, captured Lannie's attention, and threw the other end of the rope tied to Mary Lou.

Lannie caught it and knotted it over his saddle horn. The cowboys shouted back and forth to Tom, coordinating signals, then one by one they threw Tom the loop end of four lariats across the river.

Tom caught and tied them to the four corners of the wagon. His heart swelled with admiration at the determination he saw in his wife's eyes. "They will have control of all four sides of the wagon to keep it from floating downstream and will pull us right over," he said with a teasing grin. "Still scared?"

Mary Lou nodded. "I have to be honest. I'll be glad when we are safely on the other side."

Tom's eyes spoke agreement. He adjusted the twins in her lap so she could put one arm around the front of them. "Concentrate on hanging onto the wagon with one hand, hug the twins, and keep a grip on the ropes they are tied to. "Don't panic if you fall off into the water. Lannie will be watching you and if that happens, he will immediately pull you and the twins to shore. Don't worry about the twins. Just don't let go of their rope. I'll keep Buttermilk and Babe going, and we'll be over in no time."

For the first time in Mary Lou's life, two hands were not enough.

With a quick leap, Tom seated himself beside her and flicked the reins, braced his feet, and yelled, "Come on, Buttermilk. Let's go, Babe!"

Mary Lou watched the snorting, stomping horses as they gingerly responded to the guiding shouts of Tom and the cowboys. She felt the wagon ease down the sloping shore and heard the water begin its hungry rush around it. As the wheels left the ground, the current grabbed them greedily, as if to swallow them whole. For a scary moment, the river took command. Then four rhythmic, determined jerks assured Mary Lou that it was Tom and the cowboys who had control, not the river.

The twins quieted, aware of a new sensation. Tommy's eyes grew wide. He twisted his head and looked up at his father as Tom shouted encouragement to the horses. His little body stiffened, he opened his mouth, and babbled in concert with his father.

Suddenly, the ropes became taut and Mary Lou felt they were afloat. She hugged her babies tighter in her arm. "Children, this is your first boat ride." She forced a laugh and felt them relax. She glanced down at the water crawling onto the floor of the wagon and could picture it swishing around their supplies and steeled herself for the drying-out job awaiting her as soon as the wheels reached the other side.

"We've got 'em!" a cowboy shouted.

Buttermilk and Babe clambered for footing. Mary Lou

felt the front wagon wheels claw at the land and the rear wheels obediently follow. The tilt cascaded water from underneath as the rear wheels climbed onto land. They made it! A deep sigh rose in Mary Lou, then expelled in thanks to God, silently thanking the Lord for good, solid ground. They were safe on the other side.

Three cowboys leaped into the wagon, unloaded and inspected everything, and helped Tom sort out the bottom layer of wet things. The cowboys resembled washerwomen as they hung and spread dripping large and small canvases on bushes and tree limbs to dry.

Mary Lou was surprised so much had been spared. Nelson's pictures on top were perfectly safe. Bedding and clothing were all dry. Tom had packed well.

Before the boys left, they built a good fire, Tom put the coffee pot on, and Mary Lou handed out the best she had, Hattie's hand apple pies. They scarfed them down quickly, then sat around, their tin cups of coffee in hand, talking trail drives, cattle and the problem of barbed wire fences cutting up the open range.

"The worst is them sheep. They close-crop the grasses and don't leave no feed fer the cattle." Shade swilled his coffee, reached for the pot, and filled his cup. He scrunched his nose. "And besides, they smell bad."

"Well, it ain't much worse than a fightin' farmer who wants to move in and plow up the land. If'n it keeps up like this with sheep and them Eastern money bags buying up the land, we won't have no ranchin' room left."

Mary Lou couldn't understand the problem with sheep. Mama always kept a dozen or so. They supplied wool and meat. Lamb chops had always been her favorite.

The cowboys finished the pot of coffee, shouted hearty farewells, mounted their horses, and crossed the river back into Texas. Tom and Mary Lou packed up, draped the damp canvases from the bushes over the top of the wagon for the sun to dry, took their seats, and continued their journey. By late afternoon, they were deep into Indian Territory.

Mary Lou smiled at the contented babbling of the twins as they played in the kiddie coop.

Tom pointed to specks on the horizon. "Indians," he said.

Mary Lou nodded. She had never felt a fear of Indians when she was growing up on the Kansas prairie. Other than keeping an eye out for rattlesnakes, she and Jenny used to play hide and seek in the tall grass and had roamed their beautiful playground unafraid. Indians had never bothered them. The Plains Indians had usually been friendly. Mama had told Mary Lou that in the first years of 1860 when she was newly married to Pa, she had welcomed squaws and their children into their cabin. Pa objected. "Mothers are the same all over the world," Mama told him. "We get together to talk about our children." But those women had also taught Mama a lot about preservation of food, cleaning animal skins, and how to make them supple for clothing and robes.

True, there were times when they had been a nuisance. They had no sense of property. Especially, young Indian men. They were like little boys who felt perfectly free to walk into any cabin and pick up whatever took their fancy. If they had chosen something Mama didn't want to part with, the sweet way was to offer them something other than what they had taken, then bargain with them as she would a child.

Pa had always grumbled Mama was too soft on them.

"They are God's children," she had exclaimed, "and He

loves them as much as He does us." For Mama, there was
nothing in the whole world that God's love did not touch.
"God saw everything he had made and, behold, it was very
good."* Mary Lou sighed deeply. Mama had made it
sound so simple.

Tom reached over and patted her hand. "Give me one
guess, and I'll say you are thinking of your Mama."

Mary Lou turned to his touch and drank in the love pouring from his gaze. "Tom, sometimes you scare me! It
amazes me how you read my mind."

"Not true." Tom grinned. "I can tell by the look on your
face whether your mind is in Kansas or Texas."

The twins squealed behind her. She checked the kiddie
coop to see what they were doing. Tommy was sticking a
finger through a knothole on one of the barrels, then jerk-
ing it back and hugging it to his stomach. Beth did the
same. Their baby giggles made her think of tinkling bells.

The specks in the distance grew into real, live, Indians.
They were probably a half a mile or so away.

The warm day and joggling wagon lulled Mary Lou into
her reminiscence again, and she remembered the day an
Indian had staggered through the cabin door and fell face
down on the floor. Immediately, Mama had dropped to his
side to attend his wounds. She rolled him over and saw he
had been attacked and mauled by an animal and had fainted
from loss of blood.

At Mama's insistence, Pa had reluctantly fixed him a
bed in the back shed. Pa wanted him out in the barn. Mama
refused to have it so.

"If you insist on caring for him, why not out in the barn?"
Pa had asked. "Ellen, there are good and bad Indians."
Pa knew. He had ridden the plains as a young cowboy
before his accident and had been in constant contact

*Genesis 1:31 KJV

with them.

"But I can't keep my eye on him in the barn. I need to know when he needs help to show him that God loves him. The only way he can learn is if someone who loves God, loves him."

Pa gave in. He couldn't fight God, he said.

However, in 1878, when Mary Lou was eighteen, she remembered how it frightened everyone when the Northern Cheyenne escaped from their reservation at Fort Reno in western Kansas. Pa had said they were dissatisfied with poor living conditions and inadequate food rations supplied by the government. Chief Dull Knife and his discontented warriors took their squaws and children and had plundered and murdered homesteaders in their drive north through western Kansas toward their homeland in the Dakotas.

When they heard of it, Mary Lou had asked Mama, "Why do people do such terrible things?"

"Because they do not know that God loves them and will care for their needs. Jesus died on the cross for the sin of all the terrible things people do. He was God telling everyone 'I love you. Let me teach you how to love me and each other.'" As always Mama had quoted from her Bible. "For God so loved the world that he gave his only begotten son that whosoever—"* Remembering, Mary Lou smiled. Her magnanimous Mama had paused and looked into Mary Lou's eyes. "And that 'whosoever' includes Indians." A decisive nod stamped a period on her final statement.

Tom's hand pressed over hers. "You are in Kansas again."

Mary Lou nodded and they laughed. They were smiling when the Indians approached them.

---

*John 3:16 KJV

Tom held his hand up in sign of welcome, and the Indians responded with nods and raised hands. Tom made a few motions, and the Indians nodded again.

Tommy babbled from the kiddie coop.

"My son," Tom signed.

The Indians smiled wide, nodded, and nudged their horses to peer into the coop.

Tom retrieved the twins and the Indians looked from one to the other. "Twins," Tom said and held up two fingers. "Two at one time," he said, straightened his shoulders, smiled and proudly pointed to himself.

The Indians caught on and beamed, commented back and forth to each other, pointed to Tom, smiled, nodded and held up two fingers. Tom held up his hand and climbed into the back of the wagon for a small leather bag. He opened the top, reached his hand into it, and brought out some beads. "Beads," Tom said.

Four eyes brightened.

Tom dumped the beads back into the bag and held it out. The bigger Indian took them, poured some into his hand, showed his partner, spoke in his native tongue, then said, "Beads."

Tom nodded, gave them a salute from his hat brim, picked up the reins, and slapped them across the backs of his team.

The big Indian stuffed the bag into his tunic and swung his horse as the wagon began to move.

Tom grinned at Mary Lou. "Just a couple friendly Indians out for a ride. That was one of Mother's little tricks. She taught us boys the best way to show you were friendly was to give them decorations for their clothing."

Mary Lou settled back. They still had a long way to go.

three

Zack leaned forward, looked out the train window, and gave a sigh of relief. Surroundings were beginning to look familiar as the train rumbled through the outskirts of Boston. He straightened in his seat and rolled his shoulders a couple of times to ease the stiff stabbing fingers that poked his back. The ride from Texas had been interesting and exciting, but exhausting.

Of all the new modes of transportation sprouting up in America, Zack was most impressed with the new railroad systems that linked the East and West with hundreds of miles of track. Trains were smelly and noisy but a vast improvement in speed and comfort over horseback or stagecoach. And trains were changing everything, even ranching. The long cattle drives up the Chisholm Trail were now being herded to the nearest railroad, loaded into cattle cars, and shipped to eastern markets hungry for beef. He, Tom, and Smitty had been talking about the changes necessary in the Circle Z to keep it profitable, but Tom said he already had in mind what he wanted to do: raise prize stallions like Father Zachary.

The train had clickety-clacked across Arkansas, Mississippi, Alabama, and Georgia, then turned north along the Atlantic seacoast. Zack had marveled at the expanse of cotton fields in the south. Since the invention of the cotton gin, cotton was now the leading product of the entire south. Even eastern Texas had cotton fever and grew it as a viable crop. Zack gazed out the train window. America was changing everywhere.

The train blew its whistle, slowed, huffed and puffed its way toward the station platform which bustled with people waiting for passengers to disembark and make room for the next travelers.

Zack reached for his valise from the shelf above his seat and noticed his dust-laden sleeves. His coat and muddy boots were no better. *I'll stop at the hotel and clean up.* Darcy frowned on unkempt men.

His heart quickened at the thought of her being so near. His arms ached to hold her. It had been almost three months. He sighed and hoped this visit had soothed her homesickness and she would be ready and content to go home to take up their life in Texas with their son.

Zack smiled inwardly, anticipating her reaction to the surprise he had waiting for her back home—a new ranch house. He had wanted it to be farther along when he brought Darcy home from Boston, but the windows he ordered from the East had not arrived and that held up inside finishing work. Could that have been part of what had bothered Darcy? Not having a home of her own? She always talked proudly about her family home in Boston. Zack understood that. He was right proud of the CIRCLE Z. But three families in one ranch house was more like a boarding house and left little privacy except for their bedroom. He had heard that most women yearned for a home of their own. Most men did, too. A spread gave a man a solid, anchored feeling of belonging. Now, he understood why his father had expressed such feeling for the land. It added substance to a man.

Zack could hardly wait to show the new ranch to Darcy.

He had picked an area on the western side of the Circle Z. Tom and Mary Lou's ranch lay south of the main house. It was commonly understood that Nelson would inherit the main ranch house and that Mother would remain there. Had he lived, Doug's share would have been east. Zack would only need a house and a horse barn since he planned to be a lawyer. What a spread the Circle Z would be— four families and all the children! Baby Zack imaged in his mind and a lonesome ache tugged at his heart for his son.

The train came to a screeching, hissing stop. Zack picked up his carpet bag and moved along behind other passengers on their way out. When he stepped on the platform, he glanced about for a carriage that could take him to the hotel to bathe and get rid of his travel grime and Western clothing.

The elegant gentleman who emerged from the hotel and hailed a carriage bore little resemblance to the man who had entered. Zack rehearsed a scene he had anticipated in his mind. Darcy would probably be in the rose garden at this time of day. He could already feel her in his arms. Memory breathed the fragrance of sweet rose water and felt the soft touch of her lips on his. He hoped that first kiss would communicate how much he had missed her while they had been apart.

The carriage pulled up in front of an impressive, brick house surrounded by tall maple trees that cupped their leaves overhead into a huge, green umbrella. A black, iron fence stood guard. Neat, brick walks would round the sides of the graceful house to the back.

Zack twisted the doorbell and heard it ring within. It seemed forever until the door opened.

Sylvia greeted him with wide surprise. "Mr. Langdon! Land sakes!" She swung the door open. Zack removed his hat, placed it in Sylvia's waiting hand, and walked into the spacious, polished hall, a hub for numerous doors around its walls.

"It's good to see you again, Sylvia." He glanced around. "Where is Mrs. Langdon?"

"Um, she's not here, sir. She went for a carriage ride this afternoon. It is such a lovely day. . ." Sylvia's wan smile belied her bright eyes. "Come this way, sir," she said and crossed to the parlor.

Zack followed her across the shiny floor. Their footsteps echoed up the handsome, winding staircase that climbed to the second floor.

Sylvia opened the parlor door and stood aside to let Zack pass.

"Emery will take your bag to you room, sir. Miss Darcy should be home soon. They left before dinner." Her smile vanished as she turned to leave.

Zack seated himself in one of the large lounge chairs beside the fireplace. Everything looked the same. His gaze roamed the room. Zack could understand why Darcy loved this house. It had elegance. Luxurious lace curtains and draperies hung on long windows that almost reached from the ceiling to the floor, flooding the room with light. Each chair had a table companion draped to the floor with a brocade cloth and a large painted globe lamp perched on its top. Circle Z was in another world.

Impatient, Zack rose and walked to the window that faced the front porch. Roses stretched thorny fingers and clambered up trellises to bathe in the sun. Inside the fence, peony bushes drooped their large, colorful heads. Maybe if he could duplicate the porches on the new ranch, it might make Darcy feel more at home. He glanced around to see what else could be copied.

A roan horse pulling a shay pranced to a stop in front of the ornate iron fence. A young man quickly jumped out his side and hurried around to a lady in a large picture hat who shut her parasol and turned to be assisted from her seat.

It was Darcy!

The solicitous young man gently held her hand, then her elbow, and helped her to the ground. He must have said something that delighted her, because she tossed her head and laughed.

The movement was too familiar. Zack remembered how coquettish she had been with him. His insides churned, but the joy of seeing her overrode it. He heard Sylvia scurry to open the front door.

Zack eagerly turned from the window.

Darcy's tinkling laughter filled the hall. "Thank you, Charles, dear. What a delightful afternoon in the country."

Darcy's voice dripped sweetness. Her heels clicked across the wooden floor toward the parlor.

"Uh—Miss Darcy," the young man called.

She stopped, swung, and turned beguiling eyes on Charles.

Charles cleared his throat. "Miss Darcy, I would be most honored if you would allow me to escort you to the Sweetheart Ball this Friday evening." Charles moved to her side. "That is, of course, unless you are already spoken for."

Zack cleared his throat and stepped into the hall. "Yes,

Charles, she *is* already spoken for."

Darcy spun and froze.

Zack walked to his wife and embraced her. "Darling," he said and kissed her cheek. His left arm around Darcy, Zack extended his right hand to the startled young man and smiled. "I'm Zack Langdon, Mrs. Langdon's husband."

Charles' eyes shot open. Unnerved, he looked first at Darcy, then at Zack and gingerly shook the offered hand before him.

Immediately, Darcy seized the situation and turned to Zack. "Darling." She slipped from his arm, planted a soft kiss on his cheek, and smiled up into Zack's face. "I want you to meet Charles Pearce. He has been such a gracious gentleman and escorted me to a few outings so I wouldn't be so lonely."

The men shook hands.

Charles, a surface smile on his face, began backing toward the door, his hat in both hands. He nodded quickly to Darcy. "Thank you for a delightful afternoon, Darcy—" He swallowed. "I mean—Mrs. Langdon." He bumped into the door frame which cracked his smile into an embarrassed grin. "Nice to meet you, sir," he said and turned in hasty retreat across the porch, down the walk, through the wrought iron gate, climbed through his buggy from the passenger side, grabbed the reins, and snapped them. The roan responded with a leap and flopped Charles abruptly into his seat and they sped away.

Zack turned to Darcy to demand an explanation but the words stuck in his throat. His heart betrayed him. He reached and drew her into his arms. Love hunger flooded his body in response to her nearness. He closed his eyes and held her to allay the loneliness he had fought in her absence. His momentary anger evaporated with the familiar fragrance that floated around her.

Darcy let Zack hold her, then relaxed, brushed a kiss across his mouth, pushed him away, and leisurely pulled off her gloves as she swished into the parlor and casually dropped them on one of the tables. "My dear, why—why didn't you let me know you were coming? I—I would have come to meet you. Did you come by train? It must have taken days of dreary travel. Are you tired, dear? Hungry?" She turned, gazed at him for a long moment while her mouth formed a sweet smile.

Zack's gaze met hers with outrage but again his desire for her love hammered at his chest and ensnared him.

Slowly, Darcy moved into his arms and melted him with a kiss.

Zack succumbed to his need for her, pressed her close, and returned her kiss. As always, she captivated him and won.

four

Emery, the butler, entered the parlor. "Dinner is served, madam."

The men rose, escorted the ladies to the dining room and seated them.

Zack glanced at Thomas Whitney, his distinguished father-in-law who presided at his dinner table with the same confident assurance that commanded his law firm. Zack truly admired the man. He had been a forceful instrument in Zack's becoming a lawyer, which had been his dream as long as he could remember.

At the opposite end of the elegant table of fine china and shining silverware sat Sarah Whitney, a small, pretty woman who gestured and nodded commands to the servants as they moved quietly to serve each person.

Thomas tucked his white linen napkin into his neck to cover his cravat. "Glad to see you at our table again, my boy. I've missed you. I still think you ought to reconsider and come back east to be a barrister with my firm."

Zack shook his head and smiled. "Thank you, sir. You do me great honor, but what would I do with my own law practice in Texas? Its shaky legs are just settling on solid ground. I have the mammoth job and challenge to be part of bringing law and order to the West."

Darcy shot Zack a frown, then turned and smiled sweetly at her father. "Tell him now, Father."

Zack gazed from one pair of telling eyes to the other and

almost read their faces. *Wonder what juicy offer they have cooked up this time to make it attractive for me to become a part of Whitney & Marcus.* Zack had travelled halfway to Boston with a fellow lawyer who told him shocking news. The elder Joshua Marcus, partner of Whitney and Marcus, had been shot a month ago. Knowing Thomas, he would relish being in full charge.

Thomas frowned at his daughter.

Zack knew that frown. She had stepped ahead of him, and Thomas never knowingly followed anyone. An excellent barrister, a demanding boss. But he was fair and seemingly enjoyed teaching Zack. Their relationship had been good.

"In your travels, I suppose you heard my firm is standing on only one leg at this moment." Thomas lifted his chin, looked down his glasses at Zack, and cleared his throat. "I have decided to offer you the partnership. Whitney and Langdon! How does that sound to you, my boy?"

Zack hated being referred to as "my boy." Thomas did that to everyone. It accomplished it's purpose and kept everyone in line. A smile crossed Zack's face but his heart sank to his feet. From the contrived looks and grins on Thomas' and Darcy's faces, Zack surmised his father-in-law had stretched to pacify his daughter. Zack had seen that same resigned expression at the end of a few court-room sessions where Whitney and Marcus had lost the case.

Darcy reached over and seized Zack's hand. "It would be wonderful, darling, and I have found a lovely English tudor house not too far from here that would be perfect for us."

"Does it have a fenced-in yard for Baby Zack?" Zack asked. His words shattered in the air.

"Why—yes—of course, dear." Darcy forced the words through her teeth and smiled.

"I can hardly wait to see my first grandson," Sarah injected. "I ache to hold him while he is still a baby."

"He's a fine lovable boy, Mother Whitney. And his leg is growing nicely. He will probably be walking and will run to his mother when we get home." Zack smiled at his wife.

Darcy's eyes narrowed.

"Oh, did the baby fall and hurt his leg? I didn't hear about that. How serious was the injury?" Sarah asked.

"No, Mother, he was born with one leg shorter than the other. My mother knew how to massage it so it has almost grown as long as the other one. My brother Nelson was born with both legs weak and one shorter than the other. Mother massaged his legs, and Dr. Mike said she did better than any nurse. Nelson has grown strong enough to move everywhere on crutches and is even married!"

"Your mother must be a dedicated, loving woman," Sarah commented.

"She is." Zack took a deep breath, pinned his gaze on Darcy, and smiled. "I have a big surprise for you, too, my dear." *Might as well lay everything out on the table.* Zack gazed lovingly at Darcy. "Our new ranch house is raised, roofed, and ready for the windows. I was hoping it would be much farther along and almost finished when you came home. I ordered large windows like these from the East—" Zack pointed to the long graceful windows facing him, "but they haven't arrived yet. I thought they would make you feel more at home."

Darcy's clouded eyes concealed her thoughts. Suddenly, she brightened. "But, darling," her voice carried a sweet warning. "As a partner in father's law firm, we won't be needing a house in Texas."

Zack's heart sank. He should have guessed. This whole scene had been spelled out in advance—the answer cut-and-dried before he had even been asked. He glanced at his father-in-law who sat ram-rod straight behind a masked expression he had taught Zack to use to conceal his thoughts—a basic lawyer pose to buffalo his opponent. He could see through the whole ruse. Darcy had seized the opportunity of Joshua's death to twist her father's arm to arrange the offer. But Thomas Whitney had taught Zack well. He read his father-in-law's cues, which betrayed the exuberant, smooth voice. There was no doubt in Zack's mind that Thomas would gladly wiggle out from under this offer if he could.

Zack watched Darcy's face and read her obvious thoughts blazoned in a victorious I-am-going-to-win look. It tore him in half.

"Zack, are you going to accept my offer to become a partner in my firm or aren't you?"

Zack looked up from his dumpling and faced his father-in-law. He took a deep breath. "No, sir."

A pair of gray, shaggy eyebrows raised in disbelief.

Zack searched for the right words. "You do me honor in your offer, Father. I know it is a great opportunity. I thank you for even considering me." He paused, aware of bristling emotions. "My mother told me when I left Texas to come here to study law that 'once a Texas boy, always a Texas boy.' I didn't believe her then. I do now." He laid his fork on the table. "Sir, I see my job in Texas as very important also. I want to help tame an unlawful territory into law-abiding working communities like you have here in the East. We have to find some way to help Americans, Mexicans, and Indians establish laws so we can all live on the land in peace. People are moving west. The government recently made it lawful for settlers to buy up land the railroads didn't use and towns are springing up all around them. But they are boom towns and need law and order. I find it exciting to be a part of taming anarchy by established law in those places." His gaze dropped to his dumpling, and he sensed their disbelieving stares.

No one said anything.

Suddenly, Darcy rose, pushed back her chair, and faced Zack.

Zack shifted to rise from his chair but a very unladylike thrust from Darcy shoved him back into it.

Two red angry flames fired Darcy's cheeks, her mouth withdrew into a line that almost cancelled out her lips.

"Well, I am *not* going to live with Mexicans, Indians, nor Texans!" Darcy jerked her skirt around the chair and stomped out, her angry face set as if in stone. Her heels resounded like exploding cannon balls in the hallway, then she ran up the stairs.

Zack rose and bounded up after her two steps at a time.

Darcy slammed their bedroom door shut in his face.

He was angry at himself. That was no way to tell her. Surely, she understood as his wife that it should be up to him to determine where they would live. It had to be where he could make a good living. Zack shook his head. Weak point! He could make a better living here as part of the firm. But everything inside him shrivelled at the thought of accepting a partnership in a law firm in Boston.

His thoughts circled round and round. He tried to open the door. It was locked. He knocked hard to dislodge his anger and hurt. He must speak with Darcy. They could never settle anything if they didn't talk about it. Yet it angered him that Darcy and her father had tried to manipulate him. This whole scene could have been avoided if they had consulted him, given him some input at the beginning, then asked him. He knocked again—again—

Abruptly, the door swung wide. Darcy turned her back and swished to the fireplace. "We might as well get this over with," she said to the mantle, then turned and faced him.

"Darcy—" Zack began.

She shook her head. "No! I've heard what *you* are going to do. Now *I'm* going to tell you what *I'm* going to do," she snapped. Her eyes were cold and angry, her hands clenched like white claws in front of her.

Zack stepped toward her. "Darling, let's—"

"Don't 'darling' me. You have known all along how I hate ranch life. It is dirty, ugly, uncomfortable, and uncivilized. I will not live like that. I was raised to be a lady, and I cannot be a lady there."

Zack stiffened. "Then what do you call my mother? I call her a lady!"

"Don't pull your lawyer stuff on me! I will not—do you hear me?—*not* go back to Texas. Either you take Father's offer and stay here, or we will no longer be man and wife!"

Her words thrust through him like a heavy beam and snatched his breath. Zack stared at her belligerent face. "What on earth do you mean by that?"

"Exactly what I said. A man and wife are supposed to live together and share in marriage. In this marriage, I am the one who has to give up everything! There is no life for me in Texas."

Zack knew it had been very hard for Darcy on the ranch. He had felt so helpless, yet had tried his best. "That's part of the problem, Darcy, you expect me to stay here, give up the important work I am doing, and be a puppet to your father."

Darcy shook her head vigorously. "We did not say 'puppet,' we said 'partner!' Zack, you will still be a lawyer either in Boston or Texas. Don't you understand? You will still be who you are—a lawyer—doing what you love to do. I will be nothing in Texas. I would shudder to have to do all that horrible work with food your mother and Mary Lou had to do. I could not do it. I will not do it!"

We. I. An unsurmountable wall of hurt rose between them.

Suddenly, Darcy softened and took a step toward him, her arms stretched. "Zack. . .darling. . . .don't you understand there are men in Boston who would jump through hoops at the chance of being a partner with my father? I cannot believe you don't understand what a privilege has been offered you. You should be grateful that my father even considered you. He has many other men he could have chosen far better qualified than you—"

"Wait a minute. Let's get this straight. I'm beginning to catch on that this whole matter has nothing to do with me."

Darcy turned her back to Zack.

Zack grabbed her elbow and swung her around to face him. "How long did it take you to get your father to agree with you? I know your father and I don't believe this was his idea at all. I think he is happy I refused. You demanded he offer it to me. Didn't you?"

Darcy jerked to free herself from his hold.

Zack grabbed both her arms and made her face him. "Didn't you!"

Darcy twisted angrily in his grasp and turned her face away.

He pulled her tight against him and held her still. "*Didn't you?*"

Darcy refused to acknowledge him.

Angry as he was, her closeness triggered his love-hungry body and mind to consider what she was asking. *Oh God!* he cried within. *We have to resolve this. We have a son to consider.* He steeled himself to calm down. In all his life, he had never felt so helpless. His barrister training had taught him self control but he felt undone, as if parts of him were flying everywhere.

Darcy held herself rigid, ignoring him.

"Darcy—darling—I love you. A man is supposed to plan for his wife and provide for her. I plan to make money in Texas, I have already built a beautiful ranch home. After the windows are put in, you can have it decorated any way you want. If you want it to look like this house, we can order everything you like from the East and it will be just as beautiful as here, and you can be a lady." Zack felt her relax and leaned to press his lips on hers—

Darcy jerked free, walked to the fireplace, and stood with her back to him.

Zack fought his desire to follow her and enfold her in his arms and kiss away her anger. They were both too over-wrought. They needed calming time.

Suddenly, Darcy swung, faced him, and stretched to her fullest height. Rage flashed from wide eyes filled with fury.

From the very first day they met, Zack had felt this fierceness in Darcy. She loved life! She was magnificent, beautiful, charming, a delightful companion. His anger at her slackened as he remembered how their relationship and love grew. They had been deliciously happy in Boston after they were married. Their honeymoon with her sister in Georgia on the way to Texas was all he could have asked for. But when they got to Texas the transplant had been like placing a blooming flower into dry ground. He watched her shrivel and withdraw, and he hurt for her. Yet he still felt that if she had given herself half a chance, her natural zest for life would have overcome even Texas.

Darcy took a deep breath. "Zack, I'm only going to say this once." Her voice was controlled, hard, brittle. "No matter what you do, I am staying here in Boston. This is my life. I want no other." She bent her head and lifted her fist to her quivering mouth. Abruptly, she jerked her head up and gazed into Zack's eyes. "Now—now I know. We should never have been married in the first place."

Never—? Stunned, Zack stared at Darcy in disbelief.

Darcy softened and hurried on. "But you were different when you lived here. I truly loved you."

Zack flinched. "What do you mean, 'loved?'"

"You are not the same man I married. I loved and married a Boston lawyer and intended to live here where I can live in the style that is my custom." Darcy looked beyond him. In a voice cold and brittle, she spit out the words that blew him apart. "Zack, unless you take that partnership from my father, I will no longer be your wife. I will have my father arrange for a divorce."

Divorce! The word exploded in his head! A divorce was a disgrace, a failure. His wooden mouth choked out,

"You wouldn't!"

"I will!" She stood straight, chin up. Her eyes bore accusing holes through him.

Zack watched determination set her face. "But, Darcy, I love you, you love me—"

"No, I don't. I don't want to be your wife anymore."

"What about our son?"

Darcy threw her head back and laughed. "That was the worst thing that ever happened to me. I hated it. I will never have another child."

Zack sagged. *She hated having our son?* A ragged memory surfaced from those first moments when Baby Zack was born. His beaming mother had brought his new son to him. He remembered the intense father-pride he had felt as he awkwardly cradled this tiny child made up of part of him and part of Darcy. He had stood in the doorway and watched his mother return the baby to Darcy. *"Take it away,"* she had screamed.

"But Darcy—"

"But Darcy—but Darcy! Can't you think of anything else to say?" Her eyes narrowed into slits. "Get out of my sight!" she hissed. "I never want to see you again. My father will arrange everything. "Now *get out!*" she screamed.

Zack stood numb. He felt his heart crumble into pieces.

Darcy moved towards him, only to shove him aside, walked out, spit out her words, and throw them back over her shoulder. "I suggest you get the next train back to your wonderful Texas where you belong!" At the top of the stairs, she turned. "And you can keep your crippled son. I don't want him."

The winning blow. Zack watched her walk out of his

life and felt his life blood drain from him. His love for her demanded that he run after her, but his body refused the command. She had made it very clear. He felt paralyzed, his ears remained alert to hear the clatter of her heels on the staircase finally fade away.

Slowly awareness returned. Zack turned and stared vacantly around the room, seeing nothing. Finally, after what seemed like forever, his body voluntarily bent to pull his valise from under the bed. He hadn't even had time to unpack it. Just as well. Time to go home. Home to Texas . . .and their son. No. *My son.*

five

Mary Lou took a deep breath and inhaled the Kansas spring air, relishing the sweet smell of the prairie.

Tom turned to her and grinned. "Getting anxious?"

"Oh, yes!" This last day's trip had seemed endless even though Tom had made good, steady time. Mary Lou glanced back, surprised to find the twins curled together, sound asleep. "I think those poor babies feel they are resigned to live forever in that kiddie coop. You were a genius, Tom. It has given them a place to play and sleep. What would we have ever done without it?"

Tom leaned and kissed her cheek. It had been a long, hard, slow ride for Mary Lou and the twins. Cattle drives, even though they were about the same distance and more arduous, were never monotonous.

Mary Lou clasped her hands and stretched them out in front of her to relieve her backache, then shook her head and smiled. "I can hardly wait to show everyone the twins. I have a feeling they will be spoiled rotten by the time Aunt Tibby, Aunt Nelda, and everyone else passes them around. Oh, how I wish Mama. . ."

Tom put his arm around Mary Lou and pulled her close. "I don't think loving attention spoils young-uns. If that were the case, we both should be rotten by now." He gave her a squeeze and a sideways glance. "I give you a lot of loving attention. Do you feel spoiled?"

Mary Lou blushed. "Spoiled? If I am, I love it!"

Tom slowed the horses, wrapped the reins around his knee, and pulled her into his arms, his azure eyes serious. "I love you more than my own life, Mary Lou. Before I met you, I didn't know what real love and happiness were." His kiss was long and tender.

Mary Lou clung to him. If anyone had ever told her a person could love someone as much as she loved Tom and the babies, she wouldn't have believed there was that kind or that much love in the world. A sudden rush of hot tears rolled down her cheeks, and she sniffed.

Tom looked at her in surprise. "Crying? What did I say to make you cry?"

Mary Lou batted wet lashes and smiled. "Oh, you know me. I always cry when I'm happy."

Tom grinned and snuggled her within his arm.

"Papa."

Mary Lou and Tom turned. Their son's penetrating eyes stared into theirs.

Tommy grinned. "Papa," he began, then his tongue tumbled out jibberish that included an almost recognizable word here and there. His wide blue eyes stared question marks.

"Yes, son, and I pray someday you'll find a woman who will love you like your mama loves me." Tom turned a pair of identical blue eyes toward Mary Lou and received a "thank you" from hers.

Beth let out a wail as she bumped her head on the side of the kiddie coop. Mary Lou reached into her pocket and retrieved a small piece of sugar candy Hattie had tucked into a food basket. Tommy's hand shot up for his piece.

Tom spurred the horses to a leisurely trot.

Mary Lou's gaze roamed familiar terrain. They were

getting close. First, they would pass Petula Hilary's place, then Jeremy Halderan's farm, then the Martin Clay home-stead. Mary Lou hated just to ride by and wave, but she wanted to show the twins to the family first. Her old neigh-bors would understand.

Petula stood at her well, pulling the rope to raise her bucket. She paused, shaded her eyes with one hand, then raised it in a wide overhead wave.

Mary Lou waved back. "I am surprised Petula recog-nizes this wagon. Let's keep going, I'll see her later. I am anxious to get home."

Tom gave a slap of the reins to signal Buttercup and Babe to step it up.

Mary Lou squinted at a small figure way out in a wheat field guiding a plow being slowly dragged through the dirt. "For goodness sake, Nellie's still alive. That old bag of horse bones has pulled Jeremy Halderan's plow as long as I can remember. Jeremy treats that mare as if she were his mother."

"It's real easy to get attached to an animal," Tom said. "Father felt the same way about Diamond. Mother often said Father loved that big stallion more than he did her. Every inch of that animal shouted power, yet he could be as soft and gentle as a kitten. I remember the day Father first swung me up on Diamond's back all alone. He put the reins in my hands, and I think that horse sensed I couldn't have controlled him if I'd tried, 'cause he stood motionless as if he cradled a baby. As for me, I sat tall and felt like a big man."

Mary Lou warmed. Whenever Tom allowed her a peek into his life before she knew him, she tucked the golden memory in a special place in her heart until she could write it down in the memory book Mama gave her on her sixteenth birthday. Some day, things would be reversed. It would be Tom putting their boy on Tinder to create a memory for his son. Mary Lou sighed. Good memories are so important. Mama knew the value of them and had sprinkled her generously with too many to count or remember.

The Martin Clay homestead looked deserted. Probably everyone was out in a field somewhere.

As the landscape said "home," Mary Lou stretched her neck and caught her first glimpse of the speck on the horizon that would become Pa's cabin. The wagon's pace eked an eternity before it closed the gap and allowed the cabin to grow into recognizable size. Memory helpfully rushed in and put Mary Lou on Dulcie's back to relive the feel of flying in a wind that had torn at her hair, snatched her ribbons and whirled them skyward. She peeked at the twins. Beth raised questioning eyes. Her little fingers gripped the wooden bars of the coop and she swayed with the faster roll of the wagon.

"I wish I had time to clean the twins up a bit," she said to Tom. Yet, she was sure no one would pay the least bit of attention to their tousled hair or soiled, wrinkled clothes, considering their trip. Her heart began to pound. She stretched her neck to see if the barn door was open or closed. Was Pa home? Had he forgiven her? She inwardly called, *"Can You still reach his heart?"*

Tom pulled on the reins. Buttermilk and Babe slowed to a plod. They were near the end of their journey.

The door of the cabin flew open and Aunt Nelda ran out, fanning her apron and shouting, "Tom! Mary Lou! Thank God you got here safely!"

Tom jumped out of the wagon and walked around to receive the twins from their confinement.

Mary Lou lifted the top of the kiddie coop. The twins had pulled themselves expectantly to a standing position. Mary Lou scooped out Beth, handed her to Tom who transferred his daughter into the eager waiting arms of her great aunt.

Nelda hugged her close and kissed the baby on both cheeks. "Land sakes! This must be Beth! She is beautiful and looks just like your Mama." She shifted Beth and stretched out her other arm for her nephew as Mary Lou handed him down to Tom.

Tommy's wide eyes surveyed his great aunt only a second, then he turned abruptly and wrapped himself around his father.

Nelda laughed. "That's all right, sonny, we'll get well acquainted before you go back home."

Tom helped Mary Lou to the ground.

Mary Lou ran to her aunt who threw her arms around her. Beth pushed back, looked with surprise at the woman holding them, then turned and wrapped her arms around her mother's neck.

Everyone walked toward the cabin, over-talking each other's words.

"I sure had a hard time all week keeping my mind on my work. Today, I figured you had to be close if you left Texas at the time you told me in your last letter."

Mary Lou's gaze toured the cabin, barn, and fields, then turned questioning eyes to her aunt. "Is. . .is Pa home?"

Nelda smiled tenderly. "No, child. He and Glenn had a big stock shipment come in today, but he promised to come home as early as he can for supper."

Suddenly, Tommy stretched out his arms to Nelda. As she reached for him, Beth reached out toward her, too.

Aunt Nelda laughed, "I figured they would come around soon." She perched Beth on one arm and held out her other arm to Tommy. "Come on, young man. I've got two arms and this one is aching to hold you."

They trailed into the cabin and Mary Lou's home hunger feasted on this dear place, her true home. As they walked through the door a quiet peace enveloped her.

Aunt Nelda had made few changes. Mama's book shelf Pa had built on the wall still held her books. Mary Lou would love to take them home with her to teach her children when they were old enough. Mama used them when she taught Mary Lou and the neighboring homestead children as well. Her gaze touched everywhere, and Mary Lou's heart rejoiced with the comfort of being surrounded with Mama's things.

Nelda bent to put the twins on the floor. "Whew! They are two armfuls," she said and plopped down on the floor with them.

Mary Lou and Tom laughed when the twins both tried to clamber into her lap and almost bowled their great aunt over.

"And how's Aunt Tibby and Nate? Is she still stirring up the world?" Tom asked. He picked up Tommy and untangled his fingers from Aunt Nelda's hair. He laughed. "Are you sure you did the right thing when you switched grooms at our wedding?" Beth snuggled into Nelda's lap.

"Absolutely! Without our female meddling, you wouldn't have married this girl of your dreams, and I wouldn't be hugging these babies." Nelda teased.

They laughed; then Nelda wanted to hear all about their

life in Texas and their new ranch house.

"Oh, you would love it, Aunt Nelda. It has five rooms!"

"My goodness, I'd like to see it sometime."

"There will always be room for you in our home," Tom said.

"Oh, I mean to visit. My home is here with my brother. He and I are the only ones left in our family as far as we know."

With quick efficiency, the table was set, the children fed, nursed, and put on the floor with a ball of yarn Nelda gave them to play with. It lasted until Tommy was so tangled in it, he had to be rescued before he strangled himself.

Supper pots hung ready and waiting.

Mary Lou set four places at the table and only half listened to Tom and Aunt Nelda's joshing. Her ears were tuned for the familiar sound and rhythm of a well remembered clip-clop. When it reached her ears, she could sit no longer, so she rose and stood in the cabin doorway. About a half mile away a dust-cloud tail swirled behind a dear, familiar buggy. *Oh Lord,* her heart cried to God. *Let him receive me again as his daughter. May he have forgiven and forgotten my defiance and accept Tom as his son-in-law. And the babies, what will he accept them?*

Mary Lou felt Tom's presence behind her. His arms folded around her waist to steady her trembling.

Pa made his usual loop around the cabin and into the barn.

Mary Lou looked up at Tom. No words needed to be said. He let her go. She slowly stepped out the door, walked around the cabin to the barn.

As she walked in, he had already unhitched Morgan from the buggy and was guiding him out the barn door to the water trough. Their eyes met as he passed her, but he continued his chore. Mary Lou walked to the trough and stood beside it. When Morgan dipped his head, their eyes met and clung.

"Hello, Pa," Mary Lou said. A rising lump closed her throat.

"Hello, daughter," Buck answered, "good to see you."

Four words, but each one was studded with diamonds. *Good to see you.* Did that mean—?

Her father hobbled beside Morgan as he swung him around and went back to the barn. He loosened and pulled the saddle, held on to the stall, and threw it up over with one hand.

Mary Lou had always admired the way Pa managed in spite of his injury. She slid the bridle over the horse's ears and removed the bit, glancing now and then at her father. Their eyes brushed several times.

Her father never had been a man of many words. Mama always said Pa was a doer, not a talker.

"How was your trip?"

Mary Lou smiled. "Long, Pa."

Buck nodded. "It's a fer piece." He grabbed his cane and started toward the door.

Mary Lou walked beside him. Evidently he had had his say. She managed to keep her welling tears beneath the surface. It was not the right time. Too many fences to mend.

Tom stood and reached out his hand as Buck entered the room. The men's eyes met and challenged.

Mary Lou held her breath and prayed.

"Owen, you still owe them your blessing." Nelda's never-wasted words but her voice was soft, firm, and as usual to the point.

That caught Buck's attention. His gaze moved from his sister, to his daughter.

Tom stood erect, his hand still extended.

Mary Lou could almost sense the battle going on within both her husband and father. She knew Tom would stand the breech.

Tommy crawled across the floor, sat down, and looked up at his grandfather. Their eyes locked and suddenly Tommy opened his mouth and poured out a stream of gibberish.

Buck bent and smiled at the baby at his feet, then looked up, first at Mary Lou, then at Tom.

"That is your grandson, Buck." Nelda picked him up and pointed to Beth on the floor, "Twins! Owen, you are a blessed man."

Buck's eyes returned to his son-in-law, who stood with his hand still outstretched. He stepped forward and clasped Tom's hand. In a husky voice, he said, "Thank you."

Beth, sitting alone on the floor, folded her little neck back so she could look up at the giants that surrounded her and let out a wail.

Mary Lou scooped up her daughter and turned to her father. "And this is Beth, Pa, your granddaughter."

Buck's eyes widened. He stared for a long second then turned to Mary Lou. "Beth? She looks like—" His words stopped.

"Her grandmother, Ellen." Nelda finished his statement. "Come, Owen, and sit down." She lifted Tommy from his arms and Buck hobbled to his chair by the fireplace. Nelda placed his grandson in his lap when he sat down.

"Beth?" Buck's voice was noticeably shaken.

"Yes, Pa. We named her Allena Elizabeth after Tom's mother and Mama." Mary Lou placed her daughter on her father's other knee and he stared at her with misty eyes.

It was a holy moment. A peace washed over Mary Lou. *Mama, you are here. I can feel you smiling.*

Mary Lou dropped to her knees in front of her father and two children. "What do you think of your twin grandchildren, Pa?"

Buck looked from one to the other. When he lifted his head, his eyes glistened. "I wish your Mama could see them."

"Pa, she's in heaven. She knows."

Pa looked into Mary Lou's face for a long hushed moment. "I wish I could believe that."

Mary Lou's heart sang. As small a hope as it was, Mary Lou accepted it and was thankful. *Dear God, give Pa time to find You.*

The twins squirmed, and Tom stepped over to catch Tommy as he slid from Buck's knee to the floor. Beth wiggled after him with the help of her father.

"Well, now, is everyone ready for something to eat? That rabbit stew ought to be just about right."

The room broke into busyness.

Tom got chairs and tied the twins into them.

Aunt Nelda tied brand new large bibs she had made around their necks.

Mary Lou dished up large soup bowls of rabbit stew and put one at each place at the table.

Finally, they all settled.

Nelda looked to Mary Lou, then to Tom. "Would you say the blessing, please, Tom?"

Tom bowed his head and everyone followed except Buck.

His face was a mask, but the angry wrinkles in his forehead were noticeably shallower.

"Our heavenly Father," Tom began. "We thank You for Your wisdom to place us each into this family and ask Your blessing on each one gathered around this table. We thank You for healing wounds that only You can heal, for opening our hearts and pouring love into them so we can give it to each other. Forgive us our trespasses and bless this food in Jesus' Name. Amen."

When Mary Lou raised her head, she looked straight into Tom's eyes. She hoped her eyes conveyed her thanks for the love and respect Tom had showed her Pa. But she should have known.

Nelda picked up a plate of sourdough biscuits and handed them to her brother. "Here you are, Owen. I made these especially for you."

It was obvious to everyone that Buck had been noticeably moved by all that had happened. There was a touch of softness Mary Lou had only seen when Pa was around Mama. There has to be a lot of love bottled up in Pa. She looked at the twins as Nelda shoved spoonfuls of mashed vegetables from the stew into their mouths. A sudden realization swept over Mary Lou. Had Aunt Nelda ever had any children of her own? She realized she had never asked nor had she ever heard her aunt mention any.

Mary Lou sighed. *Life's mysteries grow deeper as I grew older.* For the second time in her life since Mama died, Mary Lou sensed an acute awareness of the heartache of people all around her, suffering in ways of which she was totally unaware. Yet Aunt Nelda always seemed strong, unperturbed. She and Tom were so happy. They had two beautiful children. Why was it life was so full for some but not for others? She had no answer. Something Mama said brushed through her mind. No matter how long we live, Mama had said, life's mysteries increase instead of decrease and we will never understand fully. We see through the glass darkly, the Bible says. That is why the Bible teaches and stresses that we need to learn to live by faith. No one will ever know it all.

She looked at Pa in faith. Was she imagining it, or did he look different? Had it happened before she came, or tonight when God graced the family with His peace. Whatever. Thank You, Jesus.

six

"Your Pa is going with us to Tibby's?"

Mary Lou nodded and her heart raised thankful praise to a God who could use two little babies to turn a stubborn man around and mold him into a devoted grandfather.

Nelda's face registered the pleasant surprise Mary Lou felt.

Mary Lou, Nelda, and the twins joined Tom and Pa in the barn. Pa had Morgan already hitched to the buggy. Tom had saddled Buttermilk and Aunt Nelda's Jewel. Mary Lou mounted Jewel. What a treat to sit in a saddle after the long wagon trip!

"Now you two just ride on ahead," Nelda called. She climbed into the buggy with Buck and held out her arms.

Mary Lou set the twins on Aunt Nelda's lap.

A desperate wail erupted from Tommy. The little boy wiggled in Nelda's arm and reached for his mother.

Tom mounted Buttermilk. "Here, hand him up to me. I rode half the state of Texas with my father on Diamond's back till I was big enough for a horse of my own. Come on, son."

Tommy's tears shut off as Tom settled his son in front of him. A twinkling, satisfied grin spread across his little face, and he grabbed the saddle horn.

"Let's get going." Nelda called. "Word has probably reached your Aunt Tibby from somewhere that you have arrived. She will have my scalp if I don't get you over to see her soon. Like me, she has been anxiously waiting for days."

And I can hardly wait to see Aunt Tibby, Mary Lou thought. She patted Aunt Nelda's sweet mare on her neck, gave her a nudge to get moving, and trotted up beside Tom.

"You two go ahead," Buck called. He swung the buggy around and as they started off, Beth wiggled in Nelda's lap, cried out and stretched her arms toward her mother.

Nelda waved them on. "Go on ahead," Nelda called. "I think I can handle one little girl." She snuggled Beth in her arms and talked and pointed as they rode away.

It felt good to be straddled across the back of a horse. Mary Lou would choose horseback over a wagon any day. Her old sense of freedom seized her, but she restrained herself from dashing off across the prairie to satisfy it. She heard Tom talking to Tommy as she caught up to him.

Tommy, eyes wide, settled happily with his father, stuck his little arm in the air, pointed and babbled his observations.

"That young man has discovered how to get his own way," Mary Lou remarked.

"Oh, Mama, your son has to get used to a horse as soon as he can. He will spend most of his life on the back of one."

True. Mary Lou's heart ached afresh for her father who had to give up that great freedom. What a horseman he had been! If it hadn't been for the accident, Pa would be so different. Mary Lou glanced back at the buggy. Aunt Nelda pointed up at something and had Beth's undivided attention.

When the Bradford ranch tipped the horizon, Mary Lou became as eager as her children. Aunt Tibby thought like

Mama, except Mama's softness contrasted her aunt's forth-rightness. Mary Lou admired women like Mama and Aunt Tibby. What a job it had been to settle the wilderness in their time and Mary Lou heard it now was so civilized that some women even had their well water piped into a kitchen sink with a pump. Perhaps, after she and Tom returned, they could check and see if it could be done in her kitchen. What a help that would be! Water inside the house!

As they neared the Bar-B Ranch, cowboys poured from the barn and surrounded them. Aunt Tibby banged out the front door, waving her arms. "Thought you would never get here," she hollered.

Mary Lou slid from Jewel, dropped into Aunt Tibby's arms, and allowed her ribs to be squeezed until they hurt.

"Good gracious, child, I've been looking for you for days."

Tibby turned to Tom on Buttermilk and stretched up her arms. "This has to be Tommy." She clapped her hands. "Come on, young man. Come to your Aunt Tibby and let me get a good look at you."

Tom lowered his son into Tibby's arms.

"Well! You are the spittin' image of your handsome father, you lucky young man." Tibby hugged and swung the surprised boy round. She pointed. "See? Your Grandpa Mackey is coming." Tibby turned to Tom and Mary Lou. "How did Buck receive the twins? He should be one proud grandpa!"

Mary Lou nodded. "Overwhelmed might be a better way to describe him." She hugged her aunt and son.

Tibby held Tommy up in front of her so she could get a good look at him.

Tommy stared and puckered his tiny brows.

"Shucks, I think you are better lookin' than your father!" Tibby teasingly grinned at Tom, kissed Tommy's cheek and snuggled him. "Tom, someday you are going to have your hands full chasing away all the pretty girls—"

Tom slide off Buttermilk and lifted both hands in the air. "Wait a minute. I have all the girls I can handle. I am in no hurry for him to grow up and multiply my problems."

Tommy reached for his father.

Tibby hugged him, then plunked him in Tom's arms.

Tibby spun and enfolded Mary Lou again and said quietly in her ear, "You have no idea how much I have missed you! When you left, your Mama seemed to leave with you."

Mary Lou hugged her aunt. "I know." They clung in their need for each other, then separated and watched Pa circle his buggy to the hitching post.

Tibby hurried to Nelda's side of the buggy with a welcoming smile for her little great niece.

Beth stared at another stranger and started to cry as Tibby lifted her into her arms.

"Hello, Beth. Come see me." Tears immediately filled Tibby's eyes and rolled unashamedly down her cheeks. She hugged the little girl close. "She looks just like Ellen," she said in a choked voice to Nelda.

Nelda nodded. "Yes. Owen noticed it, too."

The women walked to the Bar-B ranch house, trying to catch up on the news all at once for the past year in Kansas and Texas. The men headed for the stables.

Sudden movement in the doorway caught Mary Lou's eye. A little girl peeked around the frame, batting wide fearful eyes. When Tibby stepped on the porch, the little girl opened the door and ran to Tibby's side.

Tibby transferred Beth to Mary Lou, bent over, hugged the child, then took her hand and turned to face everyone. Undeniable delight sparked Aunt Tibby's eyes. "This is my new little daughter." Tibby glanced at Mary Lou and smiled. "I can see you are stunned. No more than I! The Lord sent me this child three weeks ago."

A daughter? Aunt Tibby? Mary Lou's mind whirled.

The smug look on Nelda's face revealed she had been sworn to secrecy to give Tibby her moment of triumph.

The girl ducked behind Tibby's skirt, peeked out shyly, then drew back.

Tibby pulled her from behind. "Come, dear, and meet your family." She stood the girl in front of her and crossed her arms protectively over her shoulders. "This is Snow Flower, my new daughter."

Snow Flower's intense frightened eyes and hair were almost black, her skin light brown.

Aunt Tibby took Snow Flower's hand. "Come inside and I will tell you about her."

Aunt Tibby's kitchen kindled memories. Mary Lou had always felt at home here. The kettle on the stove busily bubbled its readiness. Tibby made tea and they settled around the table which displayed two heaping plates of tempting sugar cookies, one with raisins and one without for the babies. Beth and Tommy were each tied in a chair and given a cookie.

Snow Flower clung to Tibby, a questioning look on her face.

"Where did you get her, Aunt Tibby? She looks Indian."

"She is Indian. Caroline Wimbley found her wandering alone on the prairie. And you know Henrietta and children. She gathered her in and was going to keep her till someone came for her, but I asked Henrietta if I could keep her till then. Big Jon said she probably become lost from her tribe when they were on the move. As far as we can figure, she must be three or four years old."

"Lost from a tribe?" Mary Lou shook her head. "Mama always said the Indians took very good care of their children. She surely knows her tribe. Did you ask her?"

"Oh, yes. But she does not speak or hear. At first I thought she couldn't understand. Then, one day, we were out in the garden. I clapped and called her name but she never looked up, turned around, or anything." The little girl stood gazing up at her new mother. Tibby cupped her upturned face in her hands, bent over and kissed her on the forehead.

Mary Lou asked, "How did you know her name?"

"I named her. Caroline said when she found her, she was carrying a handful of snow flowers. I thought Snow Flower would be an appropriate name for her."

Snow Flower snuggled closer, her dark eyes fixed on her new mother. She darted shy glances at Mary Lou.

"What if someone comes for her?" Mary Lou asked.

"Then I will have to give her up. But until that time—" Tibby smiled into Snow Flower's upturned face, "I figured the good Lord sent her to me and has given me the blessing of being her mother even though it may be only a little while." Tibby put her arm around the child. "For now, she is mine."

Tommy and Beth squirmed to get on the floor.

Snow Flower's eyes followed them as they crawled toward each other. Suddenly, she left Tibby's side, sat down on the floor, folded her legs under her, and looked at them.

The twins crawled and sat beside her. Snow Flower touched each one on the head, then sat motionless while Tommy climbed and grasped her shoulder for balance, intrigued with a new playmate.

Tibby turned to Mary Lou. "Now, tell me about your new house."

Mary Lou described the ranch, adding their plans for its future to make it a vital, joint part of the Circle Z.

Mary Lou asked, "Tell me about Jenny and Glenn. Jenny's letters sound so happy and busy."

Tibby nodded. "They are good together, Mary Lou. Jenny has made a comfortable little home at the back of the store. Glenn is talking of adding more rooms on the back to give them a full kitchen downstairs and add bedrooms upstairs to made a real home. Jenny is full of ideas and seems content."

Mary Lou laughed. "Jenny told me she never did want to be a farm woman. I agree, they need more rooms than just those two behind the store. I remember the shrinking feeling I had when Glenn and I were engaged, and he announced to me those two rooms would be our home. The very thought smothered me. I wanted to be a rancher's wife. And I am—thanks to you two." Mary Lou blew a kiss to her aunts.

Nelda smiled. "God has a way of working things out far better than our best intentions. Jenny enjoys working out in the store as well doing the postoffice."

Mary Lou relaxed. A longing to see her dearest friend nagged at her heart. It would be impossible to go to Venture today—tomorrow perhaps?

The women sat, reminisced between jumps to retrieve Tommy as he struck out on new adventures. Then Tommy took a sudden shine to Aunt Tibby who was delighted. She carried him around, talked and named him different things in the kitchen. Beth watched their every move.

Mary Lou's gaze travelled the room. Her second home when she was a little girl. A mood of nostalgia swept over her. Funny how a look, a word, a house, a land could lift up memories and make them become doubly precious. She gazed at her dear family. *I have to capture as many memories as I can to take home with me.*

Mary Lou related the events of the past year: the birth of Baby Zack, Nelson and Laura's wedding, the birth of the twins, Doug and Lily's marriage, Doug's untimely death and Lily's disappearance.

Her aunts doubled with laughter as Mary Lou told of trying to befriend Darcy and teach a city girl to be a rancher's wife. "Before we left, Zack left for Boston to bring Darcy home from a visit to her parents. They will probably be there when we return." Mary Lou spoke fondly in praise of Allena and Hattie.

"It is a busy household, believe me. I love them all, but Tom and I are glad we are in our own place."

Mary Lou got up and walked to Aunt Tibby's stove. Hers at home was just about the same. Mary Lou felt proud. Tibby and Nelda were interested and pleased when Mary Lou told them about their new ranch. A sudden burst of pride in Tom and their accomplishments welled up as she spoke of them.

The twins became fussy. No wonder. It had been a big day for them.

"I think we had better put these babies to bed," Aunt Tibby commented.

Stomping boots announced the men's return.

Mary Lou's heart swelled with unbounded joy when she saw her Pa and Tom walking and talking slowly behind Nate and a couple cowboys. Tears surged for release. If only—the words struck in her throat. How many times Mama had cautioned her. *Never say "if only this would happen—" or "if only that—" it's a weak crutch. Instead of wishful thinking,* Mama always said, *Pray!* Mary Lou's heart rose with a new sense of loss. Being home had freshened her longing for Mama. *Father,* she prayed, *I miss Mama so.*

A sudden explosive thought grabbed Mary Lou's mind. *If Mama were alive, she would be here with Pa, and I would be in Texas with Tom. We would be apart! More so.* Now, Mary Lou sensed Mama's presence wherever she went. How strange are the ways of God!

seven

Beth's whimpering wakened Mary Lou. She looked at the clock. Six already? She quietly slipped out of bed, into her wrapper, and picked up Beth. Father and son stirred. She softly touched Tom's arm so he would think she was still beside him. Mary Lou wanted him to get all the extra sleep possible. He needed it.

She stooped for the pair of slippers Aunt Nelda had made and given her yesterday. She had forgotten to bring her own. Mary Lou smiled. Mama would have commented, "But my God supplieth our every need."*

Beth stretched her arms to be picked up, then cooed and nuzzled her mother. Mary Lou shushed her and tiptoed out of the room, coaxed by the aroma of fresh coffee.

Aunt Nelda, as usual, had risen before everyone. "Best time to keep from being interrupted in my morning prayers," she had once told Mary Lou.

Nelda looked up from her Bible that lay open in her lap and smiled apologetically. "I heard Beth and would have gotten her so you could sleep, but figured I would create too much fuss and wake the whole household." She closed her Bible, laid it on the table, rose and reached for Beth.

Mary Lou shook her head. "Let me change and nurse her first, then she will play quietly. She is altogether a different little girl when she is not around her busy brother."

"Aren't most women different when they are around men?"

---
*Philippians 4:19   63

Mary Lou nodded. "I guess we are. I never thought about it before." She smiled at her aunt. "You are a wise bird."

Nelda nodded. "A wise old bird." She accented "old."

Mary Lou shook her head. "I never think of you as 'old,' Aunt Nelda. I've seen days when you ran circles around me and other younger women."

"Result of good training. My mother was a worker and expected everyone else to keep up with her. I hated it when I was young, but thankful after I married Lars. I declare, I was the envy of the neighborhood wives. Had my wash hanging out on the line first thing Monday morning before the other women was out of bed." Nelda laughed. "It became my prideful fetish 'cause it made the other women look up to me. Or, so I thought." Nelda chuckled and shook her head. "Isn't it silly how hard we work when we are young to blow ourselves up to look good, only to find out when we are older it was a waste of our precious time?"

Mary Lou laughed. "Could it be when we are young we don't have very much to offer? I know when I worked with Mama, I tired out long before she did and breathed a sigh of relief when we finished. Mama took a deep breath and began another job!"

Nelda sipped her steaming coffee. "Some wise soul said life is what we are alive to." She nodded. "Makes sense. I sure have known a lot of people who were never alive to work!"

They laughed—like old times.

Nelda set a cup of coffee on the table beside Mary Lou while she nursed Beth, then pulled up the other rocker and eased into it with her own hot cup and sipped. "Now, tell me about your new home. I hope a time will come when your Pa and I can visit."

Mary Lou's heart skipped a beat. "Oh, Aunt Nelda, do you think Pa would be able to stand a trip to Texas to see us? He would love it. Tom is breeding horses. Mama said that was what Pa set his heart to do before his accident. Tom has a special mare in foal now." Mary Lou tried to imagine Pa in their barn. "I think Pa would feel at home on the Circle Z."

Nelda nodded her head. "If there is a way to go by train, I think Owen could handle it, but never by wagon. Riding to and fro in the buggy to Venture some days troubles his back." Nelda smiled, leaned, and patted Mary Lou's knee. "I'll see what I can do. A visit might settle his mind. He would see you happy and contented, then be right proud he has Tom as a son-in-law."

What a dear woman, bless her. Not a selfish bone in her whole body. If anyone can persuade Pa, it will be Aunt Nelda. In only a day's time, Mary Lou had noticed many changes in Pa. For one, he talked. After Mama's death he had spoken few words to anyone. To see him so open and pleased with his grandchildren made Mary Lou's heart sing. There had not been any formal I-forgive-you's said between them, yet her heart told her Pa had forgiven her. Actions sometimes say what words cannot.

Beth sat quietly playing on the floor, intrigued with a string of buttons Nelda had strung for her to play with. "She might as well get the feel of woman stuff," was Aunt Nelda's comment when she gave them to her.

Breakfast smells gradually coaxed two drowsy men to appear. Tom carried his sleepy-eyed son into the kitchen. "It is a first. I had to wake up Tommy! I did not dare leave him alone cause I knew when he awakened he would find things to do where there are none." Tom sat Tommy on the floor beside his sister who was absorbed with her buttons.

Tommy proved his father right. In the short time it took the women to put breakfast on the table, Tom refereed both son and daughter and had to separate them in a do-or-die fight over the buttons. Finally, Tom tied them both into chairs and placed Beth's chair beside her mother and Tommy's chair by him on opposite sides of the breakfast table.

Buck came in and took his place. Mary Lou's heart rejoiced as Pa bowed his head while Tom said grace.

Today they planned to go to Venture. By the time everyone was ready to leave, Tom had completely emptied the wagon except for Nelson's pictures and the kiddie coop.

Bumping along in the wagon surrounded by her beloved prairie, Mary Lou took an imaginary fast ride to town on Dulcie's back. She used to make it in twenty minutes. In the buggy and wagon, it took twice that time. She thought of Dulcie in Texas and wondered, do horses get homesick or nostalgic? Had she come, would Dulcie have felt she was home? Mary Lou naively believed she would.

Tom followed far enough behind for the buggy dust to dissipate before it reached the wagon.

Tommy fussed to be in the kiddie coop to play rather than be confined to his mother's lap. Mary Lou opened the lid and put him in to play with his toy horses, resettled herself on the seat, felt her body relax, and feasted her eyes on her dear homeland. The prairie grass had grown over knee high already. She remembered one day when she was little, she and Pa had walked through grass higher than her head. Like something alive, it had slapped at her face and frightened her even though she had hold of Pa's hand. She had screamed and cried until Pa picked her up and carried her home. When older, she and Jenny used to hide in it.

Tom had told her Texas had similar prairies in the south eastern part. "I'll show you sometime," he had promised.

She squinted at the broken outline of Venture ahead on the horizon and wondered if it had changed much in the almost two years she had been gone. It didn't matter. Venture would always be the same to her. It sheltered precious memories.

As the wheels chewed up the distance and rolled into the west end of Center Street, Mary Lou waved to people she recognized. Neighbors and friends who had peopled her whole life came walking, running, smiling, and greeting them as Pa and Tom pulled the buggy and wagon to a halt in front of Mackey's Mercantile.

But it was soon obvious the star attractions were the twins.

A beaming Sarah George grabbed hold of the wagon as soon as it stopped. "Land sakes! Is this our little Mary Lou with a baby in her lap? Why I remember when. . . ."

One after another came up and said "hello," "Glad you came to visit,"—"we have missed you. . ."

Dear people, almost like family. They grew to know her, she them, as they came to the post office twice a week to get their mail. Mama had worked three days each week and at first carried Mary Lou in a wicker basket and set it on the floor by the window so she could see the birds, clouds, and sky. Her first real memory of involvement in the actual work had made her feel very important. Mama had stood her on a chair beside her and gave her the mail to hand over the counter to waiting customers while Mama searched the boxes. She knew all the townspeople's names by heart before she ever read them.

She and Mama had worked together fifteen years. When Mama's illness kept her home, Mary Lou had assumed the job of postmistress. Now these dear familiar faces, smiling and welcoming her— She fought the intrusion of a waterfall within and scolded herself. *No! Don't you dare cry!*

Jenny bounded out the front store door, waving her arms in the air. "Mary Lou Langdon! You goin' to stay in that wagon all day?"

"Jenny!" She looked beautiful! Mary Lou passed Tommy down to Tom who gave her arm leverage as she jumped to the ground.

On her way to Jenny, old friends and neighbors smiled, said, "Welcome home," "Good to see you again," patted her shoulders, and arms. Finally, the two girls came face to face smiling. Jenny propelled Mary Lou to the store. As soon as they were inside, Jenny's arms wrapped around her and squeezed hard. "Oh," she sighed, "how I have missed you."

They clung for a moment.

"Me, too," were all the words Mary Lou could squeeze out.

The store looked wonderful. Mary Lou identified Jenny's artful touch on the neat, clean shelves, shining bowls, lamp chimneys, and orderly dress good shelves. She perused the merchandise and observed that Glenn had expanded their stock to include many new items Pa never carried. More furniture, kitchen stoves, one similar to her own at home. Mary Lou took a deep breath and turned her head to the spice boxes that still permeated the front corner of the store with their pungent fragrances.

Glenn strode forward and took both of Mary Lou's hands in his. "It's good to see you, Mary Lou. How have you been?" His soft brown eyes spoke love for a dear friend.

"I'm fine. And you—Glenn you look so happy. It was glad news when we heard you and Jenny were married." She had wondered how she would feel when she and Glenn met.

Glenn's gaze searched the room till he found Jenny.

Mary Lou sighed and a long-held burden broke loose and floated away. Glenn loved Jenny! It spoke from his eyes and shined in his face when he looked at her. Mary Lou relaxed. They had both done the right thing.

People crowded the store. Buck and Nelda sat proud, holding wide-eyed, transfixed twins, overwhelmed by so many strange people.

Gradually, as Mary Lou wandered around the store, her feet turned toward her special place, the post office.

Jenny saw her and followed.

Mary Lou stepped behind the counter. It looked much the same as—no, that was the picture she carried in her mind. Her eyes opened to the present, and she discovered changes everywhere. Counters and the pigeon hole boxes had been moved, the large safe stood firmly in the far corner. How convenient, she thought, remembering how she had to carry her stamps and money all the way through the store to the back rooms where Pa had kept the safe.

Mary Lou turned and smiled at her dear friend who stood beaming with anticipation of Mary Lou's approval. "Quite an improvement, Jenny. You have made it much more efficient."

"Glenn says that if Venture keeps growing, he wants to enlarge the store. He's already ordered kitchen chairs from Chicago he saw in an order catalog to begin a small furniture section. I don't know where he expects to find room. Every available space is stuffed already." Jenny laughed. "But knowing Glenn, he will find it. Sometimes I think some of his ideas are way over his head, but we have doubled the business and with all the new people coming in and. . ."

Mama? Mary Lou's mind called. Silence.

All of a sudden, Mary Lou didn't want to look at or hear any more. Priceless memories labored to shift and reshape to accommodate the present. *Mama? I don't feel you here anymore. I don't even feel me here!*

Mary Lou turned to leave. She felt as if something precious was in danger of being snatched from her and that if she lost it, she would be destitute without it. She turned and walked out.

Jenny followed her back into the store. "Come see the back rooms, Mary Lou. The curtains you and Aunt Nelda made are still there."

True, Aunt Nelda's perky curtains hung at the windows, but Mary Lou delighted in Jenny's imaginative hand everywhere. How charming! Jenny had done so much with so little.

Mary Lou's spirits lifted. She stretched her arms wide and twirled in appreciation. "Jenny, you have done wonders to this place. And did I hear right, you plan to build on the back and make a real house with an honest-to-goodness kitchen and upstairs bedrooms?" Mary Lou hugged Jenny. "I'm happy for you. Dear friend, you have earned it!"

Jenny beamed and returned her hug.

They walked back into the store. Mary Lou checked the twins. Tommy stepped lively between two young boys and Beth stood shakily between two little girls. Obviously, they were being well watched and entertained.

She looked for Tom. He had Nelson's pictures on display. Glenn and a group of men nodded in lively conversation. Mary Lou told Aunt Nelda that she and Jenny wanted to take a peek at the new pews in the church.

Nelda nodded her head and shooed them off with a wave of her hand.

Like chattering magpies, the girls walked toward the church, stumbling over each other's words, trying to relate at once everything that had happened since they had last seen each other. They giggled at everything, the same as they used to. Yet there hung between them a—a strangeness, a barrier that had never been there before.

Mary Lou sensed Jenny felt it too. She could tell by the jumpy way Jenny talked. Of course, they had been apart for a long time, and there were so many new and different areas of change in each other's lives they each knew nothing of. . .and—

Suddenly, Mary Lou remembered Jenny's concern when her older sister got engaged and married. Jenny had said she felt as if she had lost her.

The girls reached the church, quietly opened the door, walked in, and stood together in the silence.

Memories whirled. Mary Lou's heart settled to rest as her gaze anchored on the new pew in the place where she and Mama always sat with an empty space beside them for someone new or visiting. Mary Lou inwardly knew Mama prayed that Pa would fill that place. He never did.

The big, fat, pot-bellied stove, the pulpit—all still the same. A tingling warmth ruffled Mary Lou's heart to alert her. *Mama is here.*

Her mind mentally produced highlights of her life in this sanctuary: the special honor given her when she was fourteen and chosen to be Mary, the mother of Jesus, in the Christmas pageant; high-pitched children's voices at the joyous celebration afterward when Santa stomped in with his bag of gifts, one for every girl and boy. For years Mary Lou had wondered how Santa always knew exactly how many girls and boys there were, knew all their names, handed out the exact amount of toys, and left with an empty bag.

She glanced out the window into the church yard that recalled Fourth of July picnics, and how she and Jenny always won all the running races 'cause they always ran the prairie.

Her gaze returned to the pulpit where every Sunday, Mama and Mary Lou had given serious attention to Pastor Miles as he moved back and forth waving his arms and hands through stirring sermons that took Mary Lou a while to appreciate, and now, which she was ashamed to admit, she remembered very little.

Her mind shifted to the day she was thrust into womanhood as Aunt Tibby and the women of the W.C.T.U., with faith and purpose, smashed the saloon. The exhilaration of that day vanished two weeks later in the humiliation of her wedding at the Bar-B Ranch. *I'm glad my wedding was not here,* Mary Lou mused. The unbelievable events of her wedding had made it the worst and the best day of her life.

As if reading her thoughts, Jenny's voice broke through

her reverie.

"I'll never forget the day of your wedding, Mary Lou. I felt so bad that I was in on the plan to stop your wedding to Glenn. But I knew you really loved Tom, and in honest friendship, I could not let you marry Glenn. That's why I promised your Aunt Tibby I would speak. Worst thing was, I told you I would do that very thing, remember? You liked Glenn, you said, but remember I said like isn't good enough for marriage."

Mary Lou nodded. "How well I remember and naturally, I thought of you first, then suddenly realized it wasn't your voice. Then Glenn spoke and acted like the gentleman he is."

Both women got lost in momentary reverie.

Jenny broke the silence, her voice pained. "But the bad thing was, I always sort of felt our friendship was never the same after that, Mary Lou."

Mary Lou put her arms around her dearest friend. "No, Jenny, God had His hand on all our lives. He knew my heart. He knew I loved Tom. Feeling as I did, it would have been wrong for me to marry Glenn. Besides," Mary Lou smiled, "you told me that you were sweet on Glenn, so everything worked out for the best."

Jenny heaved a big sigh, then they giggled, just like old times.

"But that's not all of it, Jenny. Remember the time you told me that things were never the same between you and your sister after she was married. That has happened to us. But it doesn't mean it is bad and will harm our friendship. We had a special little girl friendship. Everyone doesn't have one. You had lost your mother and father and I was an only child. God put us together in His plan so we could teach each other what friendship really is. All is blessing from God, Jenny. He gave us the opportunity to truly love someone who was not part of our family. When we grew up, we knew what real love truly meant. Mama always said a real friend accepts the other person's faults, good and bad, always believes the best and would rather give than get. She also told me Jesus was my best Friend. 'I have called you friends.'* She also told me that to be accepted as a true friend was the highest compliment anyone could ever pay me." Mary Lou smiled and watched Jenny's face break into a broad smile of relief.

The old familiar tingling teased Mary Lou's neck to announce a new discovery. *A husband and wife should be best friends* Why is it, Mary Lou thought, whenever you try to help someone else understand you get a better understanding for yourself?

Jenny slowly walked toward Mary Lou and looked at her. "I never thought of it that way, Mary Lou. You are right. Our friendship isn't ever going to be the same way it was. We were children then. Now we're women. It will be even better." Jenny put her hands on Mary Lou's shoulders and gazed into her dear friend's eyes, smiled and nodded. "You know what, Mary Lou? You sound just like your mama."

The statement took Mary Lou's breath away. *Me like Mama?* "Oh, Jenny." She gently took Jenny's face in her hands and kissed her cheek. "That is the most wonderful compliment anyone has ever given me."

They left the church with eyes sparkling. The old, relaxed, teasing chatter returned with a fresh knowing that the bonds of true friendship can never be broken.

---

*John 15:15

eight

Tibby Bradford and Snow Flower joined the other wagons and buggies in front of Mackey's Mercantile. Snow Flower jumped out of the buggy and tied the line to the hitching post.

On her way back from the church, Mary Lou waved to Aunt Tibby who waved back and waited on the boardwalk with Snow Flower.

Mary Lou greeted her aunt with a kiss on the cheek. "I didn't know you were coming to town today, Aunt Tibby."

"Well, I figured if I am going to see very much of you, I'll have to follow you wherever." She put her arm around her niece.

Snow Flower ran to Mary Lou's other side, slipped her hand into Mary Lou's, looked up and smiled. Her dark eyes spoke her welcome.

"She likes you," Tibby said.

"I like her, too, and I'm happy for you, Aunt Tibby. You finally got your girl."

"Why, Tibby Bradford! How are you?"

Mary Lou turned to the voice. It belonged to a tall, thin woman draped in a tiny-flowered, ill-fitting calico dress. She must be someone new in Venture. Mary Lou had never seen her before.

"Hello, Mabel. May I introduce you to my niece, Mary Lou Langdon? This is Buck's daughter. She, her husband, and family live in Texas and are visiting us for a couple weeks."

"Oh, you must be the one who used to work in the post office and had such an awful wedding." Mabel waved a limp wrist. "We just moved here from Virginia. My man wanted to come West but our money ran out when we got to Kansas, so I guess I am stuck here, but I—"

"It is nice to meet you, Mabel." Mary Lou struggled for composure. "I hope you grow to like Kansas after you are here a while. I was born here. I think it is a lovely place to live."

Mabel shrugged her shoulders. "A woman goes where her man goes whether she likes it or not." Mabel leaned over and stared at Snow Flower standing behind Mary Lou.

Aunt Tibby reached for Snow Flower's hand and moved aside a couple steps. Mabel grinned and nodded "Oh, is this the child I've heard about?"

Tibby's eyebrows lifted. "I don't know. What did you hear?"

Snow Flower ducked behind Tibby.

"Well," Mabel began hesitantly, "I heard you had taken someone in to work for you. Is it the custom in Kansas to have Indian girls work as servants? I could use one."

Aunt Tibby stretched to full indignant height. "I am sorry, Mabel, you have been misinformed. Snow Flower is not my servant, she is my adopted daughter." Tibby suppressed a smile as Mabel's eyes widened and her mouth dropped open.

Mabel's disbelieving gaze bounced from child to Tibby and she gasped, "But—she's—an—Indian."

Tibby slipped a protective arm around Snow Flower. "Yes." She stroked the child's cheek and smiled into her upturned face. "And isn't she a lovely one?"

"But—but—you got her dressed like a little girl!"

Tibby's brows shot up. "Of course. Because that is what she is—a little girl!"

Mabel's disconcerted gaze darted back and forth. Her mouth opened for a weak "Yes" and stretched into a limp smile.

Tibby moved toward the store. "Nice to see you again, Mabel, but please excuse us. I must hurry to my errands." Tibby grabbed Snow Flower's hand and walked in the store. Mary Lou and Jenny hurried behind her, discreetly trying to keep their faces straight.

Tom crossed to Mary Lou the minute she entered the store. Beth lay drooped in Aunt Nelda's arms, sound asleep. Tommy had wrapped his little arms around his father's leg and hung on, his eyes wide and starey.

"Are you ready to leave? I think it's time we got these two back to the cabin." Tom grinned, "It has been a busy morning."

"Tom, would you mind if Mary Lou rode home with me so we can visit a bit?" Tibby asked. "I have a few things to get at the store and will send her home later."

Tom nodded. "That is what we are here for, visiting."

Tommy laid his head on Mary Lou's shoulder while Tom climbed into the wagon, then Tom lifted his exhausted son into the kiddie coop, straightened his hat, waved, and slapped the reins.

Pa and Nelda followed, in the buggy, Beth sound asleep in Nelda's lap.

When Mary Lou re-entered the store, Glenn stood on a ladder hanging Nelson's pictures on a side wall.

I wish Nelson could see them displayed, she thought.

Customers commented favorably and one seemed very

interested in Mary Lou's favorite: a lean cowboy, in chaps, who sat tall in the saddle and reminded her of Tom. Perhaps knowing people were interested in his paintings would give Nelson a new incentive to keep on. Since he and Laura had married, Allena showed concern that Nelson spent so little time at his art.

On their way home before they turned south, Tom planned to go east to Abilene to take the rest of Nelson's paintings to Silas Jamison's big general store. Glenn told Tom he would keep a check on them and return the money to Nelson by mail.

"Now I will finally get a chance to talk to you," Aunt Tibby said as they climbed into her buggy.

Snow Flower sat between them and laid her head in Tibby's lap. The rocking of the buggy quickly lulled her to sleep.

"I want to hear all about Tom's family. A letter isn't the same. I gather your mother-in-law is a solid Christian woman."

"She is and has been wonderful to me from the moment I met her. But she has had one jolt after another. All three sons brought home wives and thrust them on her unannounced. When Zack came home from Boston, he brought Darcy. Then Tom came home with me. Allena graciously accepted us and treats us as one of her own. She is a loving lady, a strong woman, so nothing throws her off balance for long.

"The big jolt came a few months later when Doug brought one of the saloon girls home as his wife. He had married her before a judge in Harness the night before. She was dressed in their usual short flouncy dress, black stockings, and high lace shoes. Doug laughingly called it her "wedding dress." Allena stood stunned for only a moment and ignored her son's disrespect. Instead of showing disappointment in her wayward son, her heart reached out to Lily who put up a brave front and stood obviously nervous and uncomfortable. She ordered Hattie to get a pitcher of warm water, told me to loan Lily one of my dresses, so she could get out of her 'wedding dress,' then guided Lily to Doug's room and told her to wash and change and make herself comfortable.

"Lily returned to the kitchen looking like a different person. With all the paint washed off her face, decent clothes, and her beautiful hair piled on top of her head, her whole demeanor changed. She was beautiful! Doug said he liked her the other way."

"Lily fell in love with Baby Zack, much to Darcy's delight. Lily took complete care of him and adored him. He thrived. Darcy pretty much ignored him and treated Lily like some hired nursemaid.

"Then without saying a word, two weeks after Doug was shot, Lily disappeared, and we haven't seen nor heard from her since. We were all heartbroken and still cannot understand why she left. She had been a good wife to Doug even though he was rude and uncouth to her."

"Humph," Tibby grunted. "Too many men find themselves a good wife, then treat her like dirt." She shrugged her shoulders. "But I guess it's no different than when a good man gets stuck with a lazy, good-for-nothing for a wife."

Mary Lou chastised herself for thinking of Darcy.

"Well," she continued, "at least we know Lily is God's girl. Before we built our own house, Allena and I had devotions every morning in the parlor. One day we noticed

movement outside the door and discovered Lily standing
in the hallway listening. Allena asked her to join us. That
week the study we had selected was Proverbs 31. Allena
calls it 'God's mirror of a beautiful woman.'"

Tibby smiled and nodded. "How like our Lord to arrange that."

"Yes, and that chapter dissolved Lily into tears, she re-
pented of her past life, accepted Jesus as her Lord and
Savior and daily, God noticeably released Lily's dormant
inner beauty. Doug also noticed the change, disapproved,
and spent more time in Harness.

Tibby stroked Snow Flower's long black hair. "Does
Lily have parents somewhere?"

Mary Lou shook her head. "Mother and I asked her
about them. Lily told us she does not remember her parents. She thinks her grandmother cared for her but she
died, and that was when she became a bound child. She
was sold two times before she was fourteen; then, the man
who owned her sold her to a fellow who came by in a
wagon filled with young girls Lily's age and transported
them from one house of ill repute to another."

Tibby slowly shook her head back and forth. "That poor
girl. I've heard of the practice of selling both children and
old people who are destitute on auction blocks like slaves.
The children bring good prices 'cause they are strong and
can work, but the older people are sold to the lowest bid-
der for their keep for a year for what work they can do."
Aunt Tibby's brows pinched together. She shook her head.
"Selling any people, especially young vulnerable children,
is sinful and against God's will. The Bible makes it very
clear what will happen to anyone who harms a child, even
in the womb. Jesus says in Matthew 18:6: 'whoso shall

offend one of these little ones which believe in me, it were better for him that a millstone were hanged about his neck, and that he were drowned in the depth of the sea.' And I abhor the sinful traffic in young girls and women for the saloons. One day, we women will be able to vote, then we'll see a change." Tibby looked down at Snow Flower, whose head was nestled in her lap. "I wonder what would have happened to this sweet child if those hucksters had found her. When we discovered that she was unable to hear or speak, the good Lord told me He had sent this little girl to Nate and me to love and fill the childless voice in our hearts. Nate and the cowhands adore her." Tibby bent and kissed Snow Flower on the forehead.

Mary Lou gave high praise to Hattie then and tried to give her aunt a word picture of her new ranch house and how wonderful it felt to have a home of her own.

"Do you like it better in Texas than Kansas?" Aunt Tibby asked.

Mary Lou had to think a moment. "Not really. Different states are—different. Our home, Tom and the children being there is what makes it a special place for me."

The Bar-B Ranch came into view. Nate came out of the barn with one of the cowboys who took the horse and buggy.

"You ladies have a good time in town?" Nate asked. He lifted Snow Flower to the ground, smiled and smoothed his hand over her long, straight hair.

"Wonderful!" Tibby called, turned and motioned to Mary Lou. "I'm hoping you have time to come in for a short tea party."

The special embroidered cloth, three good china cups, saucers, and Grandmother Stafford's teapot were taken from the shelf and swept Mary Lou into a wave of nostalgia as she set the table. There had always been at least three places, Aunt Tibby, Mama, and Mary Lou. Now it was Aunt Tibby, Snow Flower, and herself. She swallowed a lump that tried hard to stick in her throat.

Aunt Tibby set a plate of her special individual fruit cakes on the table. *I'm glad that some things don't change*, Mary Lou thought.

"Did Nelda tell you we are having a barbecue tomorrow? We thought instead of you having to visit everywhere, everyone could come her to see you."

Mary Lou sighed in relief. "That will be wonderful." She and Tom had discussed how they would spread their time to see everyone.

Aunt Tibby sent a scribbled note with Snow Flower to the barn that Mary Lou would need a horse to ride back to Buck's.

They carried the dishes to the wash table. Tibby suddenly turned and gently cupped Mary Lou's face with her hands and kissed her cheeks. "The older you get, the more you remind me of your dear Mama. You are a lot like her, you know."

The comment took Mary Lou's breath. Aunt Tibby was the second person today who had told her she reminded them of Mama. Joy exploded in her innermost being. "Thank you, Aunt Tibby," was all she could say through her choked-up throat. It made her proud yet humble. To follow in Mama's footsteps. . . Her heart swelled with thanksgiving to God. She kissed Aunt Tibby, mounted and headed for home.

The ride home was exhilarating. It would have been better if she had been on Dulcie's back, but. . . As she neared Pa's cabin, a sudden strange feeling of inner detachment loosed her spirit and sent her mind soaring to Texas. She missed Allena, Zack, Laura, Nelson. . .their new home.

The next morning, Nelda and Mary Lou cooked and packed food for the barbecue and planned to leave at before ten.

"Tibby told me she wanted us there first to greet everyone," Nelda grinned. "Get ready, 'cause it sounds like she has invited everyone in the state!"

Shortly after they arrived at the Bar-B, Mary Lou recognized a familiar wagonful coming from the west. Tom and Mary Lou each held a twin, who waved their little hands at the children as the wagon came in, and they all waved back and giggled.

Big Jon pulled the wagon to a halt, jumped down, walked around and helped Henrietta to the ground. The older children one by one jumped and helped the little ones to the ground, and they formed a long line behind their mother and father in front of Tom and Mary Lou.

Henrietta swept Mary Lou into her arms in a motherly squeeze that brought tears to both their eyes, then pushed her at arm's length to take a good look at her. "You have matured, my dear. It becomes you." Hastily she took the twins, one in each arm, before they could object. "And these babies!" She kissed each one. "My, my, wouldn't Ellen be proud. They are beautiful."

Next thing Mary Lou knew, a pair of burly arms swept her off her feet. Big Jon! How many times those arms had been her solace and substitute for Pa's. Her heart swelled with gratitude and love for this man—a true man of God. Mary Lou also knew that she had not been the only recipient of his largess. Big Jon eased her down on her feet and held her an arm's length away. "Look at you! Happiness shouts from every corner of your face." His kind, brown eyes bathed her with his blessing. "I'm glad," he said softly.

Mary Lou's tears refused to stay contained. They poured down her cheeks unashamedly as she drank in the welcome and affection of this dear man. "Thank you, Big Jon," she sputtered.

He stepped aside to expose his brood.

Mary Lou couldn't get over how the ten little Wimbley children had grown. Little! Young Jon stood tall as a man, almost to his father's shoulder. Miriam, a young lady of fifteen, and. . .

One by one, each child shyly gave her smiling hugs. Caroline, almost six, threw her arms around Mary Lou's legs and looked up. "Where did you go so long? You never come over to our house anymore. Where did you get the babies?"

Mary Lou and Tom laughed. "God sent them." Mary Lou swept the child into her arms and looked at Big Jon. "Thank goodness she hasn't changed. Still the same little continuous question box."

Caroline backed off and looked seriously into Mary Lou's face and nodded. "Oh, God's gonna send you lots more, I betcha."

Henrietta reached for Tommy, then scooped Beth into her other arm. "I can't believe my eyes. Two dear babies, how blessed you both are."

All smiles, Tom and Mary Lou basked in their children's shadows.

One by one the families came, in wagons, buggies, on horseback from town, ranch, and farm.

The men sat and tended the roasting steer suspended and

sizzling over the pit while engaged in a rousing discussion of farming and ranching. As usual they came to an impasse. The farmers objected to the cattle overrunning their planted fields. The cattle ranchers complained of the shrinking grassland for grazing because of the plow.

Everyone wanted to hold the twins. Tommy and Beth were passed around and stepped high between children until they were exhausted. Mary Lou finally took them inside and nursed them. She laid them sound asleep on a blanket on the floor of Aunt Tibby's downstairs bedroom and returned to the party.

Eating, talking, and joshing went on all afternoon but the food never seemed to diminish. For these hard-working pioneers, any social event in the company of neighbors was a joyous time.

As the sun took aim at the horizon, one by one, the wagons of dear friends and neighbors departed amid waves and shouts of goodbye. When the last wagon left, everyone began the cleanup.

The Wimbleys and Jenny and Glenn stayed to help and were the last to go.

Later, in the upstairs Bradford bedroom where Mary Lou and Tom had spent their fist night as man and wife, they covered their tired, sleeping son and daughter on their double comforter floor bed. Mary Lou lifted her mind and heart in thanksgiving for all the dear families that had peopled her life for as long as she could remember. What memories flooded back in seeing them.

She knelt at the bedside, said her prayers, climbed into bed and Tom's arms.

He held and kissed her. "Have you had your visit? Are you about ready to start home?"

Mary Lou's mind travelled to Texas to their lovely new ranch house. Oh, but it had felt so good to be home.

"We should be leaving fairly soon. My mare will foal in a couple months but she was mighty big when I left home. She must be carrying a big stallion which could spell trouble. Smitty can handle everything, but I'd like to be there."

Mary Lou raised on her elbow, cupped Tom's head with her arm, and kissed him. "Anytime you say, Tom."

Mary Lou's heart wavered. This was home. Yet— She thought of their ranch, her new stove, the rolling land, Allena, Hattie. . . The last thing she remembered was the feel of Tom's soft lips kissing her forehead.

nine

Tom rolled the dripping wagon out of the Red River onto the Texas side of the Red River Station. Jake, Less, and Pete gave a holler, wound up the ropes and brought them to Tom.

"Thanks, boys, much obliged." Tom said. "Can I buy you some grub in the station?"

All three shook their heads. "Naw, we ate before ya came. 'Twern't no trouble. Anytime." They each touched their hat brims, bowed their heads to Mary Lou, then headed for the big red barn that housed the station.

Tom climbed down to check Babe and Buttermilk. Their heads hung low. Tom had driven them hard every day since they had left Abilene where they had dropped off Nelson's paintings, then headed down the old Chisholm Trail. He figured he wouldn't be meeting many herds at this time of the year.

They entered the station and the same cheerful lady who had waited on them before looked up and smiled big. "Well, now, if'n it ain't them beautiful twin babies back again." She nodded to Tom and Mary Lou. "Glad to see ya. Did ya have a good trip?" She straightened and wiped off a table. "Here, set yourselves here, and I'll get some rags to tie in them twins."

Unfortunately, the menu hadn't changed, but it was hot and surprisingly tasty. Better than trail food.

Back in the wagon, it didn't take the twins long to settle

in the kiddie coop.

Tom and Mary Lou rested on a blanket and leaned their backs against a wagon wheel to give the wagon time to dry off.

Mary Lou laughed. "I've done less in the last week than I do in one day at home, but I don't remember ever being this tired since we built our house." Her heart suddenly reached for that little ranch house on top of a knoll. "It will be good to get home."

Tom nodded. "Sure will."

The next morning both Tom and Mary Lou were up and gone early. They didn't eat breakfast at the station. Tom built a small fire, Mary Lou made coffee, and they munched on sour dough biscuits. She nursed the twins, put them in the kiddie coop, and they both lay down. *Good little travelers*, Mary Lou thought.

The warm morning sun climbed until it was overhead and hot. Tom kept a steady pace. It would take the best part of the day to get home.

"Do you want to go straight home, or stop off at the big house before we go on?" Tom asked Mary Lou.

Even though her first thought led to their house, she, as well as Tom, knew everyone would be on the lookout for them, every day, expecting them "any time" and be disappointed if they passed by.

Mary Lou shook her head. "We'd better stop at the big house. I hope there is some supper left over."

"Don't worry," Tom said. "With Hattie around. . ."

Tom rode under the CIRCLE Z arch shortly after supper time, and pulled into the ranch yard.

The wheels hadn't even rolled to a stop when Allena, Hattie, and Laura were out the door and running beside the wagon.

"Oh, thank the Lord you are here safe and sound. Our prayers are answered," Allena called.

The wagon groaned to a stop. Tom reached back into the kiddie coop for the twins. Allena's arms were already outstretched, grabbed Tommy, hugged him, and passed him to Laura. Beth ended up in Hattie's arms while Allena clasped Mary Lou and her son in her arms. "Thank God! Thank God!" she whispered. She pushed them back and looked at them with glistening eyes and swallowed hard. "How did you find everyone at home?" she asked Mary Lou.

"Wonderful."

"Good! And your Pa?"

Tom laughed. "The twins won his heart. It seems he has forgiven Mary Lou, and I've been accepted as his son-in-law. But," Tom gazed into his mother's eyes, "Buck is really a great man. We talked and I think his problem is that he misses his wife and his cowboy spirit is languishing in a buggy. I feel for him."

Mary Lou was touched and rushed her love and thanks to Tom through her eyes.

Allena nodded slowly. "I can understand that," she said. "Maybe some day he may be able to come this way." She turned and walked toward the ranchhouse. "Have you eaten yet?"

"Yes, but if it's Hattie's cookin', I'll eat again," Tom answered.

One word about food and Hattie was on her way to the kitchen. Soon heaping plates of beef stew, vegetables, and cinnamon cream pie appeared, as if by magic.

Shortly, Laura and Nelson arrived home from the

Shepards and joined them in pie and coffee.

"I have been getting Father Will's ledgers in order," Nelson remarked. "Did Zack tell you he put me in charge of the Circle Z ledgers and accounts?"

Tom nodded his head in approval. "He said you were getting very good at it. And you better start a ledger of your own. I brought home good news and—" Tom reached in his pocket, pulled out a roll of greenbacks, picked up Nelson's hand, and plunked them into it. "This is from the sale of some of your pictures from Mackey's."

Nelson's mouth opened in amazement. "You sold some!"

"Yes, and as fast as they went, you had better get busy! This is only for what Glenn sold the past couple weeks while we were there. On the way home, we went to Abilene and left ten at Silas Jamison's General Store. Glen said he would keep track of them and send you the money.

Laura jumped from her place, dropped to her knees beside Nelson, and looked up into her husband's incredulous face. "Nelson, I knew it! We all knew they were good."

THUMP! Tommy let out a scream. He had pulled himself up on a chair, then let go and fallen backwards.

Mary Lou cradled him in her arms to quiet him. She looked into his unhappy face and said, "I think we had better finish our journey and take our family home." She sighed. "And that includes me!" Mary Lou glanced across the table at Beth slumped half asleep in Allena's arms. "It has been a long, wonderful month. Time to go home."

Mary Lou climbed up on the wagon seat and was handed a twin for each arm. Suddenly, every muscle in her body complained. The seat felt like a hard rock, her back threatened to break, and the twins had never seemed so heavy.

Thank goodness Tom had fixed the road to their ranch

that she remembered so well the day the twins were born. There was still room for improvement.

As they approached their ranch house, her heart swelled with pride in Tom and Tex's handiwork. But the poor thing look dark, forsaken and lonely. Well—it wouldn't be for long!

Tom stopped the wagon in front of the house and unloaded their clothes bags and opened the door. Mary Lou carried in the weary twins. She walked to the water crock, lifted the lid and smiled. Bless whoever had thoughtfully filled it. *What do people do without a thoughtful, loving family? They miss a lot of the tender loving touches of life.* She washed her sleepy babies, and laid them gently into their own beds, then undressed, washed, pulled her nightgown over her head, loosed her hair and brushed it.

Tom came in from the barn in just his pants. He had used the barn water barrels to bathe. His red hair glistened with drops of water. Without stopping, he dropped his clothes on a chair, walked across the kitchen, took Mary Lou in his arms and kissed her. "I've been wanting to do that all day."

Mary Lou laughed. "You always say that!"

"'Cause it's true. I only feel like half a person when you aren't in my arms." His vivid, blue eyes spoke his desire. They walked around, blew out the lamps, and climbed into their own bed.

&

Mary Lou opened her eyes and turned over. Tom lay asleep beside her. Usually he was gone early for chores. Mary Lou resisted snuggling against his back. He'd earned a late morning's rest. Last night even the twins had curled up with no resistance.

She slowly slipped out of bed, grabbed her clothes, and tiptoed out. Surprisingly, the twins didn't stir.

Quietly, she made a fire in the stove, put the coffee pot on, made oatmeal to cook, and stepped to the door and swung it open.

An early pale, red-pink border edged the horizon and highlighted a pale, morning sky. Wispy, white clouds floated like veils over an upper haze of soft blue. Her heart rose in praise and prayer to God for His provision of an abundant, beautiful earth.

Mary Lou folded her arms across her breast and hugged the peaceful, delicious feeling of being home, then suddenly felt like a traitor. She had just come from home: Kansas, Pa, Aunt Nelda, Aunt Tibby and Uncle Nate, Jenny, Big Jon, Henrietta, and teary goodbyes. Yet standing here, basking in the soft light of a new day in the doorway of her own house, things began to reshape.

Her gaze roamed the roll of the Texas landscape and rested on their new barn in process when they left. Was it finished? Mary Lou's spirit again raised in praise. Tex must have completed it while they were gone, bless his heart. Had Tom noticed it when he took the wagon to the barn last night? He must have. *Why didn't he tell me?*

Her gaze threaded through the morning mist to the roof of the new house Zack had built for Darcy. She turned her head north to the main ranch house and watched wisps of telltale smoke announce that Hattie was up and cooking breakfast.

She felt Tom's arms fold around her and turned her cheek to his kiss.

He snuggled his head beside hers. "I am glad we are home."

"So am I," Mary Lou admitted. Ambivalent feelings bounced around her heart in search of a landing place.

Tom gazed across the land. "Getting rather impressive, isn't it? Best sight of all is that finished barn. Tex never lets any grass grow under his feet. I know he wants a ranch of his own someday, but I am selfish enough to hope it is not too soon."

"I think if we could find him a good wife, he might settle down around here somewhere," Mary Lou remarked. "That man wants a home of his own. His roaming cowboy days are over. He is looking to settle."

"If that is true, I would give him a piece of land to keep him on the Circle Z."

A small speck of a figure on horseback emerged from the Circle Z barn and headed in their direction.

"I bet you it's Mother!" Tom said grinning. "She has to check out to see if everything is all right. Hattie has probably instructed her to bring us back for breakfast."

Mary Lou nodded and laughed. "I will gratefully accept. I had better see to the twins." She turned and sent a smirky little smile back at Tom. "Now we'll find out what sort of prophet you are." She laughed and left.

Mary Lou found the twins hanging over the side rail of the bed. Tommy grinned. It looked as if he had figured a way to the floor. One leg over, he hung in balance.

"Well, you two look bright-eyed and bushy-tailed this morning." Mary Lou lifted, kissed each one, and sat them on the floor. Tired as she had been when she put them to bed the night before, she had taken time to find clothes in their chests for them to wear for this morning. She dressed them quickly. The oncoming hoof beats halted at the door and Mary Lou heard Tom greet his mother. She grinned.

He *was* a prophet!

The next moment Allena was at her side. "Where are my babies?" she cried and swept them both into her arms and bounced kisses off both their cheeks. Allena sat on the floor, gathered Beth and Tommy into her arms, and hugged and squeezed them till Tommy wiggled free and crawled over to his father. Beth laid back in her grandmother's arms and giggled as Allena tickled her stomach. She paused and looked up. "Hattie gave me instructions to make sure you came to the main house. She has been in the kitchen hard at work since before daylight."

"Oh, Mother, I accept!" Mary Lou responded. "And thanks to whoever filled the water crock. I'm glad to be home, but not quite ready to dive in."

To their surprise, Tex appeared leading Tinder and Dulcie all saddled for Tom and Mary Lou. "Welcome home. Glad to see you made it safe and sound. I'm invited for breakfast, let's go."

Tom settled Beth at the front of Mary Lou, Tommy in front of him and trotted up beside Tex. "Looks like you finished the barn."

"Yep. One of these days I am going to build my own."

"Yep," Tom said and grinned. "And I'm gonna help you build it."

Hattie met them all at the door and swung it wide open. "Breakfast is all ready."

Mary Lou and Allena put the twins into their high chairs.

Everyone took their place, quiet settled, and everyone bowed their heads.

"Father," Tom began, "we thank You for the gift of a new day filled with Your mercy and bounty. We pray to live so our lives are a witness to Your love and providence.

In Jesus Name—"

Everyone said, "Amen."

In the middle of breakfast, Zack emerged from the bedrooms and joined them. He talked and ate, but Mary Lou sensed something had happened. A restraint surrounded him.

"Did Darcy come home with you?" Tom finally asked Zack.

Zack bowed his head for a second. "Darcy is not coming back." He quickly forked a piece of bacon into his mouth. Tom stared at his brother. "Does that mean you won't be here at the ranch—that you are going back to—?"

Zack shook his head. "No." He paused, then spoke quickly. "Darcy will not leave Boston. She is divorcing me."

"Divorce!"

The ugly word screeched and dangled in the air.

Tom winced at the pain in Zack's eyes.

Zack fought emotion as he recounted his trip to Boston. "The basic truth is I do not want to be a Boston lawyer under any circumstances, and Darcy will not live in Texas with me." Zack's gaze held Tom's eyes a long moment before he lowered it.

Mary Lou voiced her thoughts. "But—what about Baby Zack?"

Sadness fleeted across Zack's face and she wished she had not asked the question.

"She—she does not want him. Baby Zack is mine alone."

A sad, quiet hush hovered over the table.

"I am sorry, brother," Tom said softly.

Mary Lou thought of her pa and how difficult it had been for him to lose Mama. She glanced at Zack. His eyes were focused on his plate. It would be the same with Zack. Like Pa, time would give Zack the blessing of remembering all the good things. It is the same whether you lose your loved one by divorce or death. They are gone and you learn to cope. When Mama died and left her and Pa. . .

No!—her heart suddenly cried out. It's not the same! When Pa lost Mama he still had the nourishment of her love in his heart and the memory of their life together. Darcy had stripped Zack of her love and had not only rejected him, but denied their child a mother's love as well! Oh, Darcy, do you realize what you have given up for your party life in Boston?

Zack glanced fleetingly at his mother, then dropped his gaze to his plate. In a husky, pain-filled voice he asked, "Figure out and tell me what purpose God has in this mess, Mother." His jaws clenched and released. His gaze darted back to his mother's face with an instant apology for his disrespect.

Allena's return gaze bathed her son with loving forgiveness. "Our Father has one," she answered, "but at the moment, our hearts are too full of hurt and our eyes too full of tears to recognize it." Allena drew a deep breath and let it out slowly. "When something first happens, we seldom understand why God allows it to happen to us. I am sure that Joseph in the Bible spent many hours wondering why his brothers hated him so much that they stripped him, sold him to Egyptian traders who in turn sold him as a slave. Yet, because of his integrity and trust in God, Joseph concentrated on being an excellent slave which caught his master's attention, and he made Joseph master over all his affairs."

Allena paused. "You know this story as well as I do, Zack."

Without looking up, Zack slowly nodded his head.

After a moment, she went on. "We think Joseph had suffered enough at other people's hands. Not so. Then his master's wife accused him of insulting her. Though innocent, Joseph landed in prison. But he excelled there also. Soon he was in charge again, and God gave him power to help two prisoners attain their freedom, and they promised to help him gain his.

"Unfortunately, once free, they promptly forgot all about him."

Zack stared intently at his mother.

Allena cradled his gaze. "This has always been one of your favorite Bible stories, Zack, even as a little boy."

Zack nodded slowly.

Allena continued. "Son, through all those events, Joseph had no way of knowing that God was positioning him to be the saviour of the whole country of Egypt during the horrible famine that stretched even into his homeland of Canaan. God gave Joseph power not only to save his own family from starvation, but to arrange for a reunion for family forgiveness in Egypt." Allena reached and placed her hand over her son's. "But remember, all these blessings covered one act of jealous spite which God completely swallowed in His love."

The familiar kitchen gathered unto itself the spirit of a cathedral.

"Zack, do not ask God 'why?' or wonder that He allows such things to happen. In His timing, you will live to see 'the why' and understand." Allena rose, walked to Zack's chair and laid consoling hands on his shoulders.

Zack looked up. "Thanks, Mother, I needed that." He rose, put his arms around her and held her while she released tears that ran down her cheeks in sympathy for her first-born. After Zack left, the talk around the table remained subdued for a while.

Allena and Hattie wanted to hear all about Tom and Mary Lou's trip, so Hattie poured more coffee and they sat and talked.

Finally, Tom rose and reached for Tommy. Mary Lou rose—

"Why not leave the twins with us," Allena said. "We have not seen them for so long we'll have to get reacquainted. The Lord knew what He was doing when He made children resilient. I've learned that while they are young, all they need is love and care and next to parents, grandmothers are rather good at that."

Tom asked suddenly, "By the way, where is Baby Zack?"

"Nelson and Laura took him with them to spend the night at Shepards'. Emily says since Laura married Nelson and all her children are gone, it is too quiet. Laura took Baby Zack along because Zack is having such a difficult time. She thought it might give him a rest. Also, Nelson has been working on Will's ranch ledgers. They should be home sometime this afternoon."

Tom and Mary Lou mounted their horses, waved, and trotted off.

"How about we take a little ride around the ranch so I can catch up on what has been done and be boss again? Riding around in wagons and buggies never has been my first choice. I will take Tinder's back, any day."

Mary Lou smiled. "Would you believe I was thinking the same thing! Dulcie must have wondered what happened to me. I feel as if I have neglected a good friend."

Mounted, they headed for Zack's house to see its progress. What would he do with it now? Unfinished. . . like his life right now. Mary Lou's heart went out to him in sympathy and love.

The land had shed some of her youthful spring caprice and settled down to its more mature summer work. Long, soft puffs of air teased Mary Lou's hair. She had piled it in a bun on top of her head and resisted the urge to drop it.

Tom and Mary Lou trotted alongside, each aware of a sense of freedom they had not had for a while. Moments of aloneness were rare since they'd had the twins.

Tom pointed to a grove of cottonwood trees and grinned. "Be a nice place to rest for a while and spoon a little," he said. Mary Lou blushed.

The shade and privacy offered a luxury they both needed. They tethered the horses and sat down beside the narrow stream that quietly played water music over pebbles and stones that washed their faces as the water rippled by.

Tom laid his hat aside and untied Mary Lou's bonnet. He reached back and released the hairpins from her luxurious chestnut hair and watched it tumble down her back. They laid back on a soft bed of grass in the shade and relaxed. Tom held her in his arms and kissed her eyes, nose and lips. "I knew you were my girl the first day I walked into the post office."

Mary Lou laughed. "My first look at you was the day I watched you cross Center Street and come into the post office. You never knew how I scolded myself for the feelings you evoked in me as you touched my hand when I handed you your mail."

"Ummm. You never told me about that. All I remember

is a girl with a tiny waist and the most beautiful face I had ever seen that I could not forget. Without realizing it, I had chosen the girl I wanted for a wife."

Neither mentioned how close they came to losing one another.

The sun travelled past the clump of trees, poked its warm piercing rays into the precious shade and frightened it away.

They watered the horses and walked a while, talking and sharing precious secrets that lovers store in their minds and hearts.

Tom stopped, leaned and kissed her. "We can see Zack's house another day. I have a hunch I should get back to my mare. Smitty says she shows all the signs to foal but she is too early and all is not quite normal." Tom shook his head. "She probably knows better than we do but judging from the size of her, it is going to be a big one and could give her trouble."

As they approached the main ranch barn Tex hurried out with a worried look.

"Something wrong?" Tom asked.

"Yeah, Smitty says it is way too early but she is having all the signs and thinks you may have a new colt before morning."

"Go on, Tom," Mary Lou said. "I'll stay here at Mother's with the twins for a while, then go on home. You go take care of your little mamma. I'll be praying all goes well."

Tom nodded, grinned, and swung Tinder toward his barn.

Tex took Dulcie, and Mary Lou walked toward the ranchhouse to see her own babies.

ten

Hattie finished breakfast dishes, wiped her hands on her apron, and met Allena as she entered the kitchen carrying two baskets.

"Would you be interested in going to Harness this morning, Hattie?"

"Yes, ma'am. I was hopin' we'd go someday soon. Our flour supply is runnin' low, and I need a new pair of shoes." Hattie glanced at her feet. "These I got hurt my toes somethin' awful, and they're too gone for mendin'."

"Well, Jess plans to drive into Harness this morning after supplies. I thought we would check to see what we need and go with him."

"Sugar and flour is gettin' low and—" Hattie's voice followed her into the store room and got lost.

"Make a list," Allena called. "I'll check with Laura and see if she needs anything."

Laura walked into the kitchen carrying Baby Zack. "Did I hear my name?"

Allena leaned and kissed the baby's cheek. "Good morning, sweet boy," she said and was rewarded by a two-tooth grin. "Jess is driving the big wagon to get supplies for the bunk house larder. We are going to town with him. Anything you need?"

Laura slowly shook her head. "No, nothing I can think of. I would just as soon stay here and take care of Baby Zack." Laura squeezed and nuzzled him till he laughed.

"Good morning," Mary Lou called as she entered the kitchen, carrying Tommy in her arms and Beth like a papoose on her back. She leaned over and deposited Tommy on the floor. "Whew! That walk from our house gets longer every day."

"It is not the walk, it's the weight of those twins," Allena said and relieved Mary Lou of her papoose.

"You're right. I'll be glad when they are both on their own four feet."

Allena smirked. "One of these days I will remind you that you said that."

They all laughed.

"We are riding into town with Jess for supplies. You want to go along?"

"Oh, yes, I need flour, sugar, and yeast." Mary Lou looked down at her clothes and shook her head. "Oh, I'm really not dressed to go to town."

"We are the same size," Laura said. "Change into something I have, and I will keep the twins. Baby Zack will love having somebody to play with."

Clothes changed, lists made, the three women climbed into the two-seater wagon and were on their way. As Jess swung the team around and headed toward Harness, Mary Lou waved to her children. Tommy and Baby Zack had attention only for each other. Beth watched her mother pull away, stuck out a pet lip, and wrinkled her face into a cry.

As they pulled out, Hattie called to Laura, "Don't forget to bake the bread when it's raised."

Laura nodded and turned to the children.

The day, delightfully warm, relaxed the passengers. The steady clip-clop of the horses' hooves had a hypnotizing effect. Even Allena rode silent.

Just before they reached town, Mary Lou pointed to the newly built church. "Oh, my! Look how the church has grown while we have been gone. The roof is on and the windows are in. It looks beautiful."

"Yes, doesn't it?" Allena smiled and caressed a memory. The original church had been built by Father Zack who often preached on a Sunday the travelling preacher could not make it. When the preacher moved westward, Father Zack preached every Sunday. One cold winter Sunday, a couple years after Father Zack died, someone forgot to close the stove damper. The stove overheated and exploded, igniting the wooden wall behind it and the church burned to the ground, scorching the trees surrounding it. Fortunately, one of the church families returning home from Harness spotted the fire. They saved as much as they could, ten of the precious hymn books, and fortunately, were able to carry out the beautiful hand hewn pulpit that had been crafted by Father Zachary with only its base injured from the blaze. It now sat repaired and wrapped in a large quilt in Allena's bedroom awaiting the first Sunday service in the new church. Then it would be brought into the new building and set in its rightful place by Zack and Tom. Tom, Nelson, Tex, and devoted community members had worked faithfully on the rebuilding as their time permitted. But church families still gathered together every Sunday morning at one neighboring ranch or another to worship.

"It is not the same to have church at home," Allena said to Mary Lou, "but the Bible tells us we must 'not forsake the assembling of ourselves together.'"*

Mary Lou nodded. Mama had felt the same way. She

*Hebrews 10:25

had always loved to be with fellow Christians. *It impoverishes one's soul to deny one's self the blessing of worship with fellow believers*, Mama had said.

Jess kept a steady pace and made good time to Harness. For the early hour of the day, the town bustled with people. Jess maneuvered the wagon as close to Orval Picket's Mercantile as he could.

Mary Lou, Allena, and Jess each left their list with Orval's wife, Martha, to fill. Hattie sat down in the chair beside shelves filled with shoe boxes and tried on shoes. Mary Lou searched the dress goods for some sturdy cloth to make dresses for the twins. They were growing so fast their dresses already touched the tops of their new high-laced shoes. Tommy now occasionally managed to stabilize both feet square on the floor and stood, his arms held high for balance, a self-satisfied grin on his little face.

Sudden wild shouting outside the store alerted everyone.

Jess immediately turned and ran outside. Everyone followed. A laboring horse carrying an excited man pounded through the center of town while the man shouted for Dr. Mike. In seconds, the doctor hurried through the door of the boarding house with his bag. "Somebody hitch up my buggy. Quick!" He turned to the breathless man. "Tell me what happened."

The man spoke between gasps. "Gustave Zigwald—who lives in the old Humphrey place—his two boys came told me—their father—gored by a bull—"

Dr. Mike spun to Allena. "I need you as my nurse." To Mary Lou and Hattie he said, "There are children and a sick mother to care for." He turned to the messenger. "You stay and lead the ladies to the farm."

Dr. Mike hustled Allena into his buggy and was gone.

Jess swung the wagon around and a couple men quickly assisted Mary Lou and Hattie into it and Jess followed the messenger as he took off ahead of them.

After what seemed like hours, in reality only thirty minutes, the women spotted Dr. Mike's buggy in front of a dilapidated barn. They hurried in, followed a man's moans and Dr. Mike's voice.

"Allena, hold this blanket and press."

At his command, Allena dropped to the doctor's side, replaced his hands with hers and pressed on a blanket wadded in the middle of the man's stomach.

The man lay sprawled on a blood-stained, hay-covered floor. His breathing was shallow. One leg jerked spasmodically.

The doctor moved Allena's hands for a second, lifted the blanket to expose an ugly, gaping hole gouged through the middle of his stomach. The doctor tried futilely to capture and halt the persistent flow of blood.

All of a sudden, the man convulsed into coughing, then gasped for his last breath.

Dr. Mike fingered his pulse, released it, then slowly crossed Gustave's hands over his chest. He reached for the man's hat, placed it beside him and stood helplessly staring down at his patient. "That bull's pointed horn punctured his heart. He was a good, strong, independent man. It's a miracle he was alive when we got here." He slipped a horse blanket from its drape on the stall and covered the man. He looked at Hattie and Mary Lou. "Go see Gustave's wife and two boys."

As they emerged from the barn, Hattie and Mary Lou saw two wide-eyed little boys standing in the doorway of the cabin. The older boy stretched his neck and looked beyond them for his father, then reached immediately for his brother, put his arm around his shoulder and drew him close.

Hattie placed her hand on the older boy's head. "We have come to help your Mama. Show me where she is so I can see if she needs anything."

The boy stared at her seriously for a moment, then swung and walked through a door beyond the fireplace. Hattie followed him.

Mary Lou bent over and lifted the little boy's hand. "Can you show me where there is some water?"

His large, bewildered eyes searched her for a moment, then he turned and walked to a bucket on a table with a tin cup sitting beside it.

"Thank you." Mary Lou looked around the room. "Does your Mama have any coffee?"

He frowned, then shook his head.

"Tea?"

He walked to a shelf and pointed up.

Mary Lou found two small cans. She opened one and released the pungent odor of sassafras. The other can was empty. She found a teapot, poured hot water from the hanging kettle in the fireplace and made tea. As she hunted for sugar, she noticed everything was neat and clean.

The door opened and Dr. Mike walked in with drooped shoulders, and Allena's pained expression must have signaled the boys something had happened.

The older boy straightened up and looked beyond them. "Where's my Papa?"

"Papa?" The smaller boy began to cry and moved closer to his big brother.

Dr. Mike's knees bent, he gathered a boy in each arm

and looked from one bewildered face to the other. "Lars. Wilmot. You remember your Papa talking about Jesus, don't you?"

Lars and Wilmot nodded their heads.

"Your Papa has gone to live with Jesus in heaven and tell him what good boys you are."

Wilmot's face clouded and tears etched two clean streaks down both cheeks.

Dr. Mike drew him close. "You are both going to have to be brave, little men and take care of your Mama." He turned to Lars. "You are the man of the house now and it's going to be up to you to take care of your little brother."

Lars straightened his shoulders, squeezed his trembling lips together, and nodded.

Mary Lou crumbled inside. *What will happen to this family now?*

Dr. Mike stood up, a hand on each boy's shoulder. "How is Zelda?"

"I don't know. She hasn't moved much since we came except for a bad coughing spell and she coughed up blood. Her breathing is quiet now."

Mary Lou followed Dr. Mike and the boys into the stark, neat, clean bedroom.

Gustave must have been a tidy man to keep such a good house, Mary Lou thought.

A wan, emaciated figure of a woman lay motionless on the bed.

Dr. Mike bent over Zelda, took her pulse, and gently returned her hand to her side.

Suddenly a strong, healthy cry of a baby cut through the quiet.

"A baby?" Dr. Mike looked at the boys. "Where is the

baby? Show me."

Both boys ran out into the main cabin to a box on the floor in the corner near the fireplace and pointed.

The three women followed.

Dr. Mike reached into a box and lifted a small blanket-wrapped baby into his arms. He turned with serious, questioning eyes. "Where is the baby's mother?"

Lars swung his arm in a wide sweep. "Out pickin' greens."

Dr. Mike shook his head. "Boys, whose baby is this?"

"She's mine!"

That voice!

Allena, Mary Lou, and Hattie all spun at once. Their mouths dropped open and hung, speechless.

Lily dropped her basket of greens and vegetables, crossed the room and relieved Dr. Mike of her crying child. She cuddled the baby to her, straightened its blankets, swayed back and forth, then looked up at Allena and smiled.

eleven

"She is mine." Lily's lips trembled. Her eyes sought Allena's. "Mine—and Doug's."

The incredulity of the moment paralyzed everyone and defied speech.

Allena's face grew radiant. She hurried across the room, enfolded Lily and her granddaughter in her arms and allowed her stored tears to spill down her cheeks.

Joy leaped in Mary Lou's heart and carried a prayer to heaven. *Thank You, Father. Thank You for Mother's sake.*

Lily handed the baby to Allena who gazed into its tiny face, then into her daughter-in-law's eyes. A questioning smile crossed her lips. "Have you named her yet?"

Lily nodded. "Genevieve Allena."

Allena beamed, then her brows posed a question. "Who was Genevieve in your life?"

"My grandmother, the only mother I ever knew—except you."

Dr. Mike turned to the boys. "When did Lily get here?"

Lars shrugged his shoulders. "She comes and helps Ma."

Allena's mouth dropped open in disbelief. "You mean you have been here—this close—all this time and you didn't—?"

Lily shook her head. "Oh no!" Lily pulled out a chair. "Come, sit down at the table and I'll explain everything." She smiled at Mary Lou. "I see you found the tea. Good."

"Not for me, Lily." Dr. Mike said. "I haven't had the

chance to tell you that Gustave is out in the barn, dead."

Lily gasped a sharp intake of breath. "Gustave dead?" She bent, cupped her forehead in her hand and pursed her lips. "I bet it was that cantankerous, old bull he wouldn't get rid of! Zelda always said that crazy animal would get him someday."

Dr. Mike nodded. "He did. Looked like the bull turned on him when he entered the stall, gored him, and ran. From what I could make out, the point of the bull's horn pierced his heart."

Lily's eyes misted, she glanced at the boys and shook her head. "Oh my, what will this poor family do without him?"

Dr. Mike picked us his bag. "Leave his body where it is for the time being. It's covered in the closed stall. I'll tell the townspeople. Someone will come and help you prepare him for buryin'."

"All I really need is someone to help dig the grave and say a few good words on his behalf. Zelda is too sick. . ."

Dr. Mike nodded and grabbed his bag. He cupped his hand under the chin of each wide-eyed boy. "Take care of your Mama and help Lily." He strode to the door and left.

Lily moved into the bedroom to check on Zelda.

Mary Lou placed cups and spoons around the table ready to fill with tea.

Lily returned to the table, poured tea, sat down and smiled at everyone. Her gaze asked patience from the three pairs of unbelieving, questioning eyes that followed her every move.

"Lily, where did you go when you left us?" Allena asked.

"Back to Harness where I came from."

Allena sucked in a short, quick breath.

Lily answered Allena's question before she asked it. "Oh, no, Mother." She shook her head. "I couldn't go back to the life I had before I married Doug." Lily stared lovingly at Allena. "I assure you, Mother, I have been with no man since my husband. Doug is the father of Genevieve. I went to the only person I could trust, Glenna, who took me under her wing the first day I was brought to the saloon. I was seventeen, and terrified. The first thing she said to me was that I didn't belong there. I knew it. I didn't want to be there, but I had no choice. I was bound to the man who brought me."

A heavy silence pressed the room.

Lily took a deep breath and continued. "Doug had never paid any attention to me, then one evening, he jokingly told me he was going to marry me. No man had ever mentioned marriage to me before. But the more I thought about it, the more I realized that it could be my escape from the life I hated. Because once I was married I would belong to my husband by law, and all the man who owned me could do was ask Doug to pay my price."

"Then one night Doug asked me again. I thought he was joking so I said 'yes.' He took my arm and led me out of the saloon just as I was. Doug woke up the judge, he married us, and in the morning, he piled me into his buggy and drove to the Circle Z. Mother, I don't know whether you can understand this or not, but for the first time in my whole life, I felt free." Lily gazed from Allena to Mary Lou. "I fully expected Doug's family to completely reject me and order me out, so I began planning how and when I could leave, and where I could go."

"Lily, did you have any love for my son at all?"

"Yes, after we were married, I believe I did. At first,

from some of the things he said and did, I thought he married me for spite. For some reason, he seemed like a driven man and quickly angered. Yet, once in a while he'd show me his loving side. If it hadn't been for that, I would have left long before I did.

"But what floored me the most, you all accepted me and treated me like family. It made me suspicious.

"Then one day out of curiosity, I wondered where you and Mary Lou disappeared every morning after breakfast. So one day, I followed you to the parlor, stood outside the door and listened to you during your morning prayer time and when you prayed for the family, you included *me*. I felt terrible 'cause I realized I was using all of you for my convenience same as Doug had used me." Lily bowed her head. "After Doug's death, I knew I couldn't say. Without Doug, I didn't belong."

"Did not belong!" Allena stared in disbelief. "Lily, the Lord allowed us to read your heart and showed us what kind of girl you really are. We love you, Lily. When Jesus saved you, you became part of God's family and our family. We were devastated when you left and even went to the saloon to find you, but one of the girls told us you were not there."

"That was Glenna, and she told you the truth. I wasn't there when you came. When I left the Circle Z, I wandered and slept in the woods, then stumbled across Gustave's barn and hid here until he discovered me. Zelda's illness had not yet put her to bed, so I worked for my keep for a few weeks. My morning sickness told Zelda I carried a child. I had suspected it, but refused to think about it. What would I do with a baby? I stayed here and helped Zelda for a month, then went to see Glenna. Two weeks later, she had found someone about forty miles away who needed a nursemaid for their children and hid me until she could find a way to get me out of town."

Lily's eyes filled with tears. "When Glenna told me you two had come to that house to find me, I couldn't believe it! You knew what I had been. Why. . . ?"

Allena shook her head. "Lily, we are not interested in what you *have* been. You are no longer that girl. We came for the Lily you became the day you asked God to forgive you. You are not that old girl anymore, you are a new creature in Christ, Lily, and you were a model daughter-in-law and loved my son, who was very difficult to love." Allena paused. "Forgive me, Lily, but I must ask. Did you know you were with child when you left?"

Lily shook her head. "No, I wasn't aware of it when I left the Circle Z. I just stayed here until I heard from Glenna, then left."

Mary Lou rose and replenished the tea.

Sudden choking and coughing from the other room raised Lily from her chair, and she sped to the bedroom.

Allena sat staring into her teacup. "Who is going to take care of this family?"

"Lily, probably." Mary Lou almost sensed Allena's mind churning and surmised she would want her new grand-daughter and Lily at home—

Allena rose and went into the bedroom with Lily.

Mary Lou poured some hot water into a small basin of cool water, washed the dishes, and strained her ears to hear the words Lily and Allena quietly spoke in the bedroom.

"I must ask you what you have in mind, Lily," she heard Allena ask.

A long pause preceded Lily's answer. "I know what I feel I should do, but—"

Silence.

"What *should* you do, Lily? What is God saying to you in your mind and heart?"

Mary Lou's ears stretched to capture their soft words.

When Lily spoke, her voice betrayed inner turmoil and pain. "Dr. Mike said Zelda is too sick to leave alone. And the boys? How could they manage? Lars is five and tended the animals when his father was gone. But Wilmot is only three, a sweet little boy and a good helper. They are both good boys. Gustave taught them well—"

Mary Lou stopped washing the dishes.

"But it is out of the question that they could tend their mother—and—they are too young to be alone—and—" Lily kept talking to avoid the obvious answer. Her voice faded into a whisper.

Mary Lou also knew the answer. She knew Lily felt obligated to stay and care for Zelda and the boys.

Silence cloistered the room, only to be shattered by Zelda who convulsed into a siege of coughing and cried out, "Got . . .halp me! Oh. . .Fodder Got. . . halp me."

Allena suddenly leaned and spoke softly into Zelda's ear.

Zelda sucked in a gasp of air and released it in a "Yesssss."

Footsteps and someone knocking on the door roused Mary Lou from her evesdropping. It was Jess.

"'Scuse me, ma'am, but with the ride back and all—it's gettin' close to noon—I gotta cook dinner for the boys. Is Miz Langdon ready to leave yet?"

"I'll see." Mary Lou crossed the kitchen to the bedroom. Before she reached it, Allena emerged.

"Yes, Jess, I know. I want you to take Hattie and Mary Lou with you and go back to the ranch. I am staying until Gustave is buried, which should be tomorrow. Then—"

Lily stepped out of the bedrooms with Genevieve in her arms and stood beside Allena.

Jess stared, mouth open.

Allena laughed. "You can close your mouth, Jess. It really is Lily you see."

Lily nodded and smiled. "Hello, Jess, it's me."

Jess's gaze moved back to Allena. "Y-yes, ma'am. It's just I was surprised—"

"We, too, Jess."

He bobbed his head and consciously forced his attention to Allena and a wide grin spread across his face. "Yes, ma'am!"

Allena nodded. "But now, I want you, Hattie and Mary Lou to go on home with the supplies. Lily and I must stay here and do what we can. Tell Tom where we are, about Mr. Zigwald's death, and that we will stay her till after the burying tomorrow. If he can't come himself, tell him to send two wagons and bring lots of quilts and pillows. He can take them off the beds, if he needs to. Tell him Mrs. Zigwald is very sick and is willing to come home with me so we can nurse her back to health. We are also bringing her two little boys."

Jess nodded. "Yes, ma'am."

As the ranch wagon rattled away, Allena turned to Lily and smiled. "Don't you think it might be a good idea for us to see to gathering Zelda's and the boy's clothing together and be all ready tomorrow when Dr. Mike sends someone out to help with Gustave's funeral? Then when Tom comes, we will be all ready to move to the Circle Z."

Lily melted into tears, stumbled forward, and threw herself into Allena's arms and sobbed.

Genevieve, squeezed between them, protested her tight quarters and squalled.

The two mothers burst into laughter, backed away, and mingled their tears with their daughter and granddaughter on her soft, pink wet cheeks.

twelve

A late afternoon sun descended its steps toward the western horizon when two packed wagons slowly rolled under the CIRCLE Z arch, carrying precious cargo.

The kitchen door flew open, and the whole family poured out.

Mary Lou, Tom and the twins, Hattie, Zack holding his son, Laura and Nelson, all stood with welcoming grins.

The first wagon stopped. Tex leaped from the driver's seat and ran around to assist Allena.

In one sweeping motion, Allena laid Genevieve in Tex's arms, placed her hand on his shoulder, her foot on the hub of the wagon wheel, and jumped to the ground.

Tex held the baby gingerly out in front of him.

Amused, Allena laughed. "She will not bite you, Tex."

Tex reddened. "I know, ma'am, but I never held such a little one before."

"Well, you had better get used to it. This ranch is beginning to blossom with them." She relieved Tex of his charge, and he moved to the other wagon and helped Lily descend.

"Thank you, Tex." She smiled and watched him as he lifted each boy to the ground.

Lars and Wilmot immediately plastered themselves to Lily.

Zack carried Zelda into Allena's bedroom. The minute he laid her down, a coughing spell seized her. Finally, exhausted, the poor woman sank back on the pillows and focused blurred, grateful eyes on Allena. "Got—bless you," she said in a forced whisper and slowly closed her eyes.

Lily had taken Genevieve, Lars, and Wilmot into her old bedroom, so Mary Lou carried her twins, followed by a tottering Baby Zack, into the room to meet their new playmates. "My, how your family has grown. With only one bed, Lily, where is everyone going to sleep?"

Lily shook her head and laughed. "Lots of room. I'll make the boys a bed with blankets on the floor. That is where they have slept most of their lives anyway. Maybe later, we can make them a real bed. Genevieve sleeps with me."

Baby Zack walked forward, stood in front of Lily, and stared up at her. Whe he caught Lily's eye, she looked at him and smiled.

"Baby Zack?" she said in a shaky voice and stooped to her knees. "Do you remember Lily?" Tears dampened Lily's lashes and she stretched her arms for him.

Baby Zack's two-and-a-half-year-old questioning eyes stared at her for a minute, then hesitantly walked into her arms.

Lily sat down on the floor, tears streaming down her face, and rocked him. "Oh, Baby, how I have missed you."

"Ma-ma?" came a tiny voice from deep within.

Lily looked up at Mary Lou through her tears and laughed. "I don't know whether that means he remembers me or not."

Lars and Wilmot circled them, then sat down on the floor beside Lily.

Tom knocked on the door, peeked in, and grinned. "Room enough for a man in here?"

Lily raised her tear-filled eyes. "Absolutely!" her shaky voice answered, "—if you want to sit on the floor."

Mary Lou reached to take Baby Zack, but he clung to Lily's neck and wouldn't let go.

Tom helped her to her feet and put his arms around them both in a brotherly hung. "I'm glad you're home, Lily. We have all missed you." He tickled Baby Zack in the neck. He ducked his face into Lily's shoulder. "Especially this fellow."

Mary Lou's heart alerted her to one of life's special moments, and she tucked it away in her heart's room for remembrance of priceless memories.

Tom leaned over Genevieve who stared back at him with the wide, dark eyes of his brother. "She has Doug's eyes," he said softly.

Lily nodded. "I've noticed that too," She unglued Lars and Wilmot from her side and touched their heads. "And this is Lars and Wilmot Zigwald."

Tom squatted in front of the boys who looked like they were ready to run. He held out his hand. "Hello, there, cowboys. My name is Tom Langdon, what's yours?"

The boys backed up. Wilmot slid behind Lily and hid his face in her skirt. Lars leaned against her and bravely stared. Tom smiled and nodded his head. "It's all right, fellas. We'll shake hands tomorrow." He rose quickly and grinned. "Father always said he should have built a double-sized ranch—one side for us to live in, and the other half for Mother's strays."

Just like Mama, Mary Lou thought.

"I'm proud to be one of her strays," Lily said softly. "There is no way you could imagine how thankful I am to be here."

Tom glanced at Mary Lou and grinned. "We found that out this spring as we traveled; there really is no other place quite like home." He turned to Mary Lou. "Is there?"

Mary Lou's head nodded agreement, and she tried to stretch home from Texas to Kansas. This time she didn't get very far.

A galloping horse and rider pounded into the yard. "Tom! Tom! Quick! Get to your barn right away."

Tom rushed out the door, jumped on Tinder, and was gone.

Lily looked concered. "Something wrong?"

Mary Lou shook her head. "I hope not. He and Smitty have been nursing Tom's favorite mare who is too early to foal. I hope nothing happens to that colt. Poor Annie. Tom says it is going to be a big one and has hopes it will be the first of many of his champion stallions. He wants to breed them like Father Zackary." Mary Lou laughed. "Having babies seems to be the same whether it is human or animal. Birthing is an anxious waiting game." She remembered the day the twins were born. Poor Annie. Mary Lou lifted a prayer for her.

Leaving Genevieve asleep in the middle of the bed surrounded by pillows, Mary Lou picked up Beth under one arm and Tommy under the other, Lily carried Baby Zack, held Wilmot's hand, and called to Lars to come. Lars stretched to his full manly height and walked beside her.

They trooped to the kitchen, tantalized by the familiar smells of Hattie's cooking, and all of a sudden, realized how hungry they were.

"How's Zelda?" Lily asked Allena.

"Sleeping quietly. The trip was a big ordeal for her. Rest is the medicine she needs right now."

Hattie worked as usual, like two people. She sliced cold beef, stirred her pot of bean porridge hanging on the fireplace as she passed by on the way to slice up two whole loaves of bread. Each woman as she entered the kitchen assumed a chore: set and reset the table as the number constantly changed; open a quart jar of pickled beets; stir the fried apples and onions; mash the potatoes, cut the raisin pies. When all was ready, Baby Zack followed Lily on her way out to ring the dinner bell.

Zack rode in, dismounted, and tied his horse to the hitching post.

"Supper's ready," Lily called to him.

"Good! I'm ready." Zack said. He picked up Baby Zack and positioned the rope between him and Lily, and they rang the bell, to the little fellow's delight.

Mary Lou saw a glow in Lily's eyes and a smile on her face as she walked through the door with Zack and his son.

If Lily missed the mention of Darcy's name in the usual course of conversation, Mary Lou felt relieved she had not asked about her. She would learn soon enough.

A horse and rider clattered into the yard. Tex burst through the door and waved his hat over his head. "Miz Langdon!" He looked to Mary Lou and Allena. "Tom sent me down to getcha both. You gotta see this. Annie just gave birth to a colt *and* a filly! Come quick!"

The impact of the news hung a moment for comprehension, then prodded everyone into action.

Supper forgotten, Mary Lou mounted Victor, and Zack mounted behind her.

Allena called to one of the cowboys for Black Beauty— "Bareback!"

When Mary Lou ran into their barn, Tom stood in the stall, his arms around Annie's neck, stroking her, softly talking to her, his face filled with awe.

On the floor of the stall, in the hay, were two dark-brown, struggling animals who did not even seem to be aware of anything except the fact that they needed to get up. Each tried, but their wobbly, uncooperative legs could not manage the right angles, and each time, they toppled back to the floor.

Mary Lou gazed in wonder. "Oh, Tom, they are beautiful. I have never seen twin foals before."

Tom's pride could not be contained. He swooped Mary Lou into his arms, twirled her and sent her skirts flying; then, he kissed her in front of everyone! "The Lord did it again, Mary Lou! Gave us a hundredfold! I was too stupid to see it. I had my mind set on one." Tom tucked Mary Lou into the crook of his arm and grinned. "Whatdaya know! The Lord sent a colt for Tommy and a filly for Beth."

Smitty stood at the back of the stall with a satisfied grin propped by weary lines of hard labor. "I have been around horses all my life, and this is the first time I have seen twin foals born, let alone a colt and filly." His eyes beamed the contentment of a job well done.

Mary Lou gazed at Annie's babies, smoothed her soft neck, and felt a kinship. "You and I have something in common, Annie. I know exactly how you feel."

Everyone laughed.

Annie stood, her head hung low, periodically nuzzling, licking, and whinnying to the helpless, struggling, brown things at her feet.

An overwhelming sense of the almighty greatness of God

enveloped Mary Lou. *The spark that is brought to life through birth is beyond our comprehension,* she mused. *Life is so common. It is everywhere, in sky, in sea, in land, in us, until we regard it lightly and live in frippery as if it will last forever.*

Suddenly, a recall from one of Pastor Miles sermons rose from deep within Mary Lou. *"Live each day as if it is the only day you have to live. Appreciate and use each moment because you will never be able to live it again."*

Allena smiled broadly and looked wistfully at Tom. "Wouldn't your father have been proud?"

Tom looked into her eyes. "Mother, I think he is."

Zack rached his arm across Tom's shoulders and gave him a solid pat.

Watching the three, Mary Lou warmed at the love and appreciation between this woman, her sons, and the proud lingering memory of father and husband. She had admired it before. And today, Mary Lou viewed an even deeper glimpse into Mother's magnanimous heart. With no hesitation, in one day, she had gathered in a desperate family, had given unlimited love and acceptance to a confused daughter-in-law who blessed her with the little baby girl she had always longed for. She had also gathered into her large heart two little fatherless boys to love and watch grow as she had her own four sons.

Mary Lou smiled, remembering how Allena hesitated to relinquish her tender baby, Nelson, her special talented child into whom she had poured her own artistic life. With fresh insight, Mary Lou realized the shock of having three of her four sons dump three unknown wives, whom she had graciously accepted, on her.

What a woman! Same breed as Mama. *Oh Lord, You*

have surrounded me with models of godly women. Not only Mama and Mother, but Aunt Nelda, Aunt Tibby, Henrietta. I want to be one of their number. May I bless my husband and children with my life as these strong God-fearing women have blessed me.

thirteen

Mary Lou climbed out of the wagon and lifted the twins to the ground. They both clung to a wagon wheel for balance, then she led a twin in each hand, and they tottered to the kitchen door. Baby Zack squealed as the twins wobbled in.

"Good morning, Hattie, how is Zelda?" Mary Lou asked.

Hattie shook her head. "We thought we lost her last night, then she rallied. Miz Langdon says it'll be a miracle if she lasts the day. She hasn't said a word, eaten anythin' or opened her eyes for two days. Poor dear, her breathin' grows more shallow with each breath. Allena's with her now."

Allena's head appeared in the kitchen doorway. "Zelda is calling for Lily and the boys," she said and disappeared.

Hattie hurried outside, called the boys, and they came running from the barn, followed by Lily.

Lily guided Lars and Wilmot to their mother's bedside and stood with her arm around each one.

Lars, wide-eyed, gazed at his mother.

Wilmot darted frightened eyes, first at his mother, then at Lily, then at Lars.

Allena leaned near Zelda's face. "Zelda? Lars and Wilmot are here with Lily to see you."

Zelda slowly turned her head and blessed her boys with a weak loving smile. "Lars—take—care—of—your—little—brother." She gasped for breath between each word.

"Yes, Mama," Lars said and wiped his wet face on his sleeve.

Lily lifted and held each boy so he could kiss his mother's cheek.

Zelda's shaky hand raised, caressed and blessed each one. "Good—sons—my—boys—"

Lily leaned over Zelda. "Yes, Zelda, and don't worry, I'll take good care of the boys. You just rest now and get better."

Zelda's blurred eyes searched for Lily, found her, and smiled faintly. She blinked a slow greeting with her eyes, stared at Lily, inhaled, and released a deep breath with her thanks. "Dunka." Peace settled on her face and her breathing ceased.

Allena picked up her wrist, felt the pulse at her neck for a moment, then shook her head. "She's gone. Her suffering is finished. Zelda has gone to be with her 'Got.'"

The boys clung fearfully to Lily. She stooped, enclosed a boy in each arm, and gently laid her cheek against each one. "Boys, your Mama has gone to be with Jesus and your Papa, but I promised your Mama I'd take care of you. You are my boys now."

A reverent quiet embraced the room as each woman prayed for Zelda's departed soul and her two orphaned boys.

Tex offered to ride into Harness, inform Dr. Mike and help dig a grave beside Gustave. Lars clung to Tex and pleaded to go with him. Finally, Lily gave permission and they rode off, Lars' legs stretched across the saddle, his back pressed against Tex's broad chest.

Tom and a couple of the cowboys made a burying box, and by late afternoon, the funeral procession slowly began

Zelda's last ride.

Hattie stayed at home to care for the twins and Baby Zack. When they all returned, a hot supper was ready and waiting.

The family gathered around the table. Lars and Wilmot stood back until Lily sat, then each boy gingerly slid into a chair on either side of her.

Tom stood, bowed his head. A hallowed quietness descended on all. "Our Father, we thank You for this day and all it has brought forth. In times like these, You make us all more aware of how dependent we are upon You and appreciate what a gift You give us in every person's life. We ask Your blessing not only upon this meal, but upon each life seated at this table. May we honor You daily with our living." He paused as if he would continue, then finished with a quiet, "Amen."

Later, in bed in their own house, Mary Lou lay awake long after Tom's breathing had relaxed into the slow cadence of sleep. The funeral had rekindled memories of Mama and a fresh realization of how fragile life really is. Alll the way home, each person had ridden subdued. Even Lars and Wilmot had seemed caught in the finality of the moment when they had stood beside the graves of both parents, barely aware of the seriousness of the occasion. Wilmot had clung to Lily's and Lar's hands, Lars had held Wilmot's hand and clung to Tex, their eyes darting silent questions from the graves of their parents to the faces of their new family around them. They had timidly followed directions and tossed their shovelful of dirt upon the box that held their mother. Now, in retrospect, Mary Lou felt it seemed almost callous to have ridden home, sat down immediately to a good meal, discuss the general activities of the day, and those planned for tomorrow as normally as if death had never visited.

No matter what—life goes on! The thought shimmered in Mary Lou's mind. Mama? Or was it God Himself who called her to attention? In afterthought, Mary Lou sensed its great truth. In all circumstances, life is on-going, surges past death and moves on without a backward look.

Mary Lou lay in reveries, remembering a day when Mama told her how God made the trees and flowers. Mama had said their only real reason for living was to produce seed peculiar to the parent plant. At the end of their season, plants released their seeds to fall into the arms of Mother Earth who nurtured each seed in its propensity to grow into the likeness of the former life. Mary Lou remembered how precious corn and wheat seeds were to the homesteaders in Kansas. Seeds were considered golden treasure, sustenance to the life of all families.

Is this what life is all about? Spending your life for the next generation? She thought of Allena who insisted that at her dinner table, Tommy, Beth, and Baby Zack's high chairs be placed at the corners on either side of her so she could nurture these little extensions of her sons, Tom and Zack.

Mary Lou thought of Nelson and Laura who had sat in a glow of happiness in the expectation of their first baby.

Yes, Lord, no matter what, life does move on. Mary Lou turned over in bed, reached her arm around her husband and cuddled his back. He stirred and wrapped her arm in his. Mary Lou lifted a prayer of thanksgiving and praise to her Father in heaven and slept.

The rays of the morning sun teased her eyes awake. Tom was gone. She dressed hurriedly and peeked in at the twins.

Beth say playing with her rag doll, Tommy lay under his bed pulling out the straw in the mattress.

Mary Lou poured oatmeal and water into a pan and set it on the stove to cook, set the table, and grabbed a hand of each twin.

"Come on, childen, let's see where your father is."

They started the slow walk to the barn. Tommy's balance had grown to the point where he insisted on trying to run and usually ended up in a heap. He kept twisting his little hand from his mother's to venture out on his own. When they reached the barn, he wiggled free, ran through the barn door, fell flat on his face and screamed.

Tom appeared, leading Tinder, stopped, picked up his son and straddled him over Tinder's back. The tolerant animal swung his head around, nickered at his passenger, and followed Tom to the corral door. Tom retrieved his teary, smiling son and released Tinder into the corral.

The family moved to Annie's stall. Like their own twins after they were born, Annie's babies took a lot of care. Especially now. They walked back and forth under their mother's stomach and tried to nurse constantly.

Tom grabbed the colt, pulled him away, and guided the filly to its mother. "He's a glutton. He'd starve his sister if I didn't interfere."

Tommy squealed with delight when Mary Lou guided his hand to pet the colt. Beth mimicked her brother, stretched her hand, touched the soft warm hair, withdrew her hand, and wrinkled her nose.

Tom smoothed his hands over the colt's back and rump. "He has great form, strong chest and neck. Even from his small start, he is going to be a fair-sized animal." Tom nodded toward the filly. "And she is going to grow into a sleek, trim young lady." He came out of the stall and picked up Tommy.

Mary Lou picked up Beth and they walked from the barn toward the ranch house for breakfast.

"Have any idea what we can name these critters?" Tom asked.

"No, but the names will come. What were you going to name just one?" Mary Lou asked.

"Uh—kind of thinking—Valiant."

"I like that." Just before they reached the ranch house, Mary Lou laughed. "What about Adam and Eve?"

Tom threw back his head and roared. "I like that! Adam and Eve it is!"

The smell of the oatmeal tweaked their hunger as they entered the kitchen.

Tom sniffed the air. "I'm ready!"

Mary Lou dished out the oatmeal, fried bacon and eggs, sliced bread, and sat down. Tom said grace.

"When do you think the church will be done?" Mary Lou asked.

"It is done for all practical purposes. Will Shepard had some of his boys worked on new benches yesterday. I think Mother is hoping we can hold the first church service within the next couple of weeks. After breakfast, let's ride down and talk to Mother."

fourteen

Zack walked out the ranch door and waved as Tom guided the buggy into the yard. "Was on my way up to see you!"

Tom reined the horses, jumped out and lifted the twins from Mary Lou's lap to the ground.

"Mother and I were talking about having the first church service this coming Sunday. Think the church is ready enough?"

Tom nodded his head. "I don't see why not. Still some finishing to do, but not enough to keep from having church."

Allena came out the kitchen door and stooped, opened her arms wide, and the twins waddled across the yard into her arms. She hooked one under each arm, hung them on her hip, and swung around and around. The twins tinkling laughter matched hers. She set them on their feet, and they clung dizzily to her skirts.

"How about us taking the pulpit to the church this afternoon and setting it up?" Zack asked his mother.

"No." Allena said. "That pulpit doesn't enter the church until the first congregation is there to see it brought in."

By the determination in their mother's face, both boys knew no argument would be considered.

"We will drive it there the day it is to be taken in," Allena announced. "When it enters the church, it should be carried to its rightful place and set permanently."

Zack nodded. "I see your point. All right, we will aim to have the inside of the church finished, and we will get the pulpit on the wagon and take it next Sunday."

"And keep it wrapped in the quilt." Allena led the twins to the kitchen door.

During the week, the ladies of the church, Emily Shepard, Allena, Mary Lou, Lily, and many of the surrounding ranch wives, cleaned furiously and banished the dust and building debris and set the benches in place, ready for Sunday. By dinner time, they were finished and unpacked huge baskets of food for both themselves and the men at work on the outside finishing.

Zack, Tom, and Nelson had rubbed the pulpit to a high sheen and lifted it into a wagon, safely wrapped in Allena's quilt and clean horse blankets, and parked it in the barn overnight. By Sunday, the drivers of the wagons were ready, dressed in their best clothes, with directions from Allena that whoever drove had to go to church and could participate in the church picnic planned for after the service.

Sunday morning, Mary Lou slipped out of their ranch door early and tramped through damp range grass to a place where she'd spotted spring wild flowers profusely in bloom. She gathered a huge bouquet to take to church. Yesterday, she had opened Mama's trunk, lifted out one of Mama's special vases and packed it carefully in one of her picnic baskets. She carried the bouquet into the cabin. Tom and the twins were waiting for her.

"Where did you go so early?" Tom asked when she entered the ranch door.

She lifted her bouquet. "I thought it would be nice to have some fresh flowers in front of the pulpit for the first Sunday. Mama always took flowers in a vase to church when they were in bloom."

Tom pulled her into his arms and kissed her. "From

what I've been told about your Mama, you grow more like her every day."

The words brought tears to Mary Lou's eyes. More than anyone else, Mary Lou had hoped to be the sweet, loving wife and mother her Mama had been to her and Pa. She also wanted to transfer to her children the inner joy of love and appreciation of God's world that Mama had given to her.

Sunday morning dawned, and the sun sprayed its warm rays across the sparkling dew and whisked it away in a vapor.

Buggies, wagons, and men and women on horseback made their way to the church for its anointing day. By the time the pulpit was to be brought in, the benches were full. Some wise souls had even brought milking stools for their children, and set them along the side walls to leave the center aisle clear.

In the left front corner stood a shining new organ donated by the Shepard family after they found out the new school teacher could play one. No one had seen her yet. Old Anna Whitney, the former school teacher, who had to quit because of poor eyesight, offered to board her free so she could have a companion in her old age.

The churchyard of Harness Valley Church, as it had been named, began to fill with wagons, buggies, and saddled horses.

Allena and family had been given the first two rows on the right side of the church. The Shepard family sat left front.

A sudden hush followed a tall, elegant lady in a blue dress and hat who gracefully walked down the center aisle to the front.

Emily Shepard rose, greeted her, and turned to Allena. "Ruthella, I want you to meet my dear friend and closest neighbor, Allena Langdon."

Allena rose in anticipation.

Emily beamed. "This is Miss Ruthella Truesdale, our new school teacher from Virginia."

"My dear, it is a pleasure to meet you," Allena said.

Miss Truesdale bowed her head in greeting. "I've heard many good things about you, Mrs. Langdon. I'm happy to meet you."

Allena smiled and turned to her family stretched out along the bench and introduced each one. When she introduced Lily and the two boys, the teacher's eyebrows raised.

Smiling at Lars, she said, "Do I see a young man who might become one of my students?" she asked.

"Yes, he will," Allena answered. "He's Lars Zigwald."

Miss Truesdale smiled at Lars and his gaze darted from side to side, then he stared down at the shiny toes of his shoes.

"Emily, if Miss Truesdale is not sitting with you, I would be glad to have her join us. We seem to have more space available on our bench than you do."

Emily laughed and looked at her family's two full benches with only one space left for her next to Will. "I agree." She turned to Miss Truesdale.

Miss Truesdale nodded. "Thank you, Mrs. Langdon. Now if you will excuse me, I do believe it is time to begin service." As she walked to the organ, one of the Shepard boys scurried behind to man the organ pump. Soon, the sweet notes of "To God be the Glory,"* filled the room. When she played it a second time, the whole congregation lifted their voices in a hearty song.

---

* "To God be the Glory," Fanny Crosby, 1820-1915

Everyone on the Langdon bench shifted to leave room for Tom, next to Mary Lou. Allena moved and left two spaces at the end of the bench at the center aisle, one next to her for Miss Truesdale to sit during the sermon, and the end seat for Zack after he and Tom brought down the pulpit.

Will Shepard rose, stood before the congregation. The buzzing murmur faded. "Friends, neighbors, it seems right and proper, before we bring in the pulpit, that we all stand and thank the good Lord for this new church."

Feet shuffled and everyone rose.

Will bowed his head. "Our Father, we're much obliged to You for this fine new church. The men have done a good job buildin', and we praise God for each one and their willin' work. Thank You for Miss Truesdale to play the organ. And now, Lord, we want to place the last piece of furniture, the pulpit, all that is left of our old church, and we thank You for the good memory and preachin' of Your man, Zachary Langdon, who made this pulpit and fed our souls every Sunday morning with Your Word until he went home to be with You. And we thank Ya, Lord, for his son and our friend, Tom, who will carry on in his father's footsteps and explain Your Word to us. May this church become a holy place that honors You. Amen." Will stepped forward and sat down on the end bench space next to his wife, Emily.

Zack and Tom carried Father Zachary's pupit down the center aisle and placed it in its proper place.

Mary Lou set her vase of flowers on the floor in front of the pulpit.

Zack sat down on the end of the bench, while Tom stepped to his mother who gave him the large pulpit Bible. Tom carried it to its place and slowly turned its pages to his text.

Before Tom began his preaching, Miss Truesdale slid quietly into her place between Allena and Zack on the bench.

Tom's message began in the first chapter of Genesis. "The first verse tells us the earth was without form and void and God made all things new. . ."

The congregation sat in hushed attention while Tom told of God's work of creation and the creation of man and woman. "And God gave us the strength to create our good life out of His earth, here in the state of Texas. Now, in this church, we used the abilities He gave us to make a house in which to worship Him. All our God asks of us is that we obey His laws in the Bible so He can spread His blessing among us as we work together in love and peace. Yes, we all contributed with our abilities, hands, effort, energy, and devotion. But may we never forget that this building is only a man-made wooden building until we, God's people, who are His church on this earth, walk through those doors. Then it becomes "Church." May God favor us with His blessing."

Miss Truesdale resumed her place at the organ and the congregation lustily sang "Oh God, Our Help in Ages Past."*

Afer a short prayer of dismissal, the parishioners poured out of the church and in no time at all, the men had rolled barrels off their wagons, set them up, and laid boards across them for serving tables. As fast as the men made them, the ladies covered the boards with beef, fish and fowl, pies, cakes, puddings, and an endless variety of fresh fruits, vegetables, pickles, and peculiar specialties.

---

* "O God, Our Help in Ages Past," Isaac Watts, 1719

Clean, old blankets and quilts dotted the ground, filled with nibbling, chatting neighbors and friends. The children ate on the run in their delight to be with all the playmates. Lars and Wilmost stood off to one side and watched while Zack and Lily joined in helping some of the children play "London Bridge Is Falling Down." Lily finally coaxed Lars and Wilmot to join in and was rewarded by two little boys who suddenly learned how to laugh.

fifteen

Summer passed quickly, consumed with caring for land, crops, animals, and children.

Tex walked into Tom's barn to put Annie and the twin foals out into the small corral. He hung on the fence and grinned at them as they awkwardly sprawled their long, front spindle-legs to enable their noses to reach the ground and nibble grass.

Movement way down at the main ranch house caught Tex's eye, and he smiled. Lars raced toward him ahead of Lily. Wilmot and Baby Zack walked beside her as fast as his short legs allowed. Tex waved and Lily waved back.

Lars arrived breathless and spewed a stream of chatter that gave no chance for Tex to say a word.

Tex took his hand, and they walked backed to meet Lily and the other boys.

By the time Lily reached the barn, she was puffing. "For the life of me, I can't imagine how Mary Lou manages carrying those twins back and forth from the main house." Her gaze turned to Tex. "The boys wanted to see the baby horses, and it's such a beautiful morning I couldn't resist a walk with them."

Tex resisted the urge to assist Lily under her elbow, but when she approached, he settled for a walk at her side.

The boys skipped ahead and hung through the lower rails on the corral, giggling and pointing to the "baby horses."

Lily and Tex rested their elbows on the top, leaned and

watched the foals feebly jump after their mother as she ran to stretch and exercise her legs.

Lars looked up at Tex. "Can I ride that baby horse?"

Tex grinned. "Not yet. He's too little to hold you."

Lars shook his head. "I'm not very big."

"Well, he has to be a grown-up horse before even a little boy can ride him."

"When I grow up, then will that baby horse be big enough for me to ride him?" Lars asked.

"Oh, yes," Tex grinned and tousled the boy's hair.

Lars climbed on the second rail, hung on to Tex, stood tall and looked Tex in the eye. "I'm gonna be a cowboy just like you when I grow up."

"All right, boy, and I'll teach ya." Tex turned and grinned at Lily as she joined him. "That is—if I'm around here that long."

Lily's mouth opened in shock. "You planning on leaving?"

"Well, I've been saving my money so's I can buy a piece of land of my own." He side-glanced Lily. "I've always had a hankerin' to run my own place."

"Don't most men?" Lily asked.

"Maybe so, but I know some cowboys lot older'n me who can't shake the wanderin' dust out of their feet."

Lily and Tex both leaned on the rail and stared straight ahead.

"Well," Lily began softly, "I've known a few women, too, who aren't much interested in taking on the work of a man and family."

Lars looked up at Lily. "Wilmot and me are your family, ain't we, Lily?"

Lily tapped each boy's shoulder and grinned. "You

certainly are and I'm glad."

"Is Baby Zack your family, too, like us?"

"Well, sort of, but he really belongs to Zack."

Tex shifted his feet, his eyes riveted straight ahead.

Lily shot a quick glance at Tex. "Well, come on boys. Let's see what Mary Lou and the twins are doing, then we have to go back down and help Mother and Hattie work the vegetable garden."

Tex turned his full gaze on Lily. "Yeah and guess I'd better get to my chores."

Both headed opposite directions.

Lars hung back. "I want to go with you, Tex."

Lily grabbed Lars' hand and pulled him with her. "Tex has work to do, Lars."

Tex swung around. "Oh, Lars can come with me, if he wants. Maybe learn a thing or two."

Lily's gaze met Tex's. "Sure he's no bother?"

"No, ma'am! I enjoy his company."

Lily gave Lars a pat on the back to push him toward Tex. "I know he enjoys yours. Talks about you all the time."

"Yeah?"

Lily nodded. "Says he's gonna be a cowboy, just like you."

Tex's face reddened. He turned and motioned his arm. "Come on, boy."

Lars ran to Tex and began a ceaseless barrage of chatter that only faded as Lily walked to see Mary Lou.

Lily peeked in the open door. "Hello! Mary Lou?" No answer broke the stillness, so she led Wilmot and Baby Zack around the house and spotted Mary Lou, hoe in hand, working a row of vegatables.

Lily laughed. "Those poor plants don't stand a chance with the help you've got."

When Tommy saw Wilmot, he squealed and ran willy-nilly across vulnerable rows of tender vegetable plants.

Mary Lou straightened up, wiped the moisture off her forehead with her sleeve, placed her hands on her hips and surveyed her garden being trampled by her twins. She dropped her hoe, grabbed them and hung one on each hip and wound her way up between the rows. "I guess I'm pushing it. Tommy does more pickin' than he does plantin'." She grinned at Lily. "Someday, and soon, I hope."

They laughed and walked to the shady side of the house. Mary Lou sighed. "Glad you came. I'm ready to set a spell."

The twins immediately each took one of Wilmot's hands and waddled beside him. Baby Zack fell in line. Tommy babbled a stream of jibberish, but Wilmot seemed to understand and put a word in here and there.

Mary Lou and Lily fixed cold vinegar-sugar tea for everyone. Wilmot took a sip, scrunched up his face and went "Yaack." The women laughed and gave him a plain cup of water.

Lily stared into her cup, then suddenly looked up at Mary Lou. "Has Tex said anything to you about leaving?"

Mary Lou searched Lily with an intensified gaze. "Yes. In fact, when we were building this house, Tex helped me put up the curtain ropes in the bedroom. I gathered from his comments, he has a hankering to find a wife and settle down."

Lily's brows raised. "Oh? Did he mention any particular one?"

"No, he just said he'd like to settle down, but couldn't find a good woman. I told him the best place to find one was in church."

Lily laughed. "He must not be very interested, or else he's given up. I don't see him in church every Sunday."

"Maybe he's found her." Mary Lou noticed a shadow cross Lily's face and smiled.

They chatted and sipped and kept the children corraled.

Lily rose and heaved a deep sigh. "Well, I'd best get back. Genevieve will need a feeding. That's the one thing Mother can't do. She does everything else for her."

Mary Lou caught a tone of hurt in Lily's voice. "Does that bother you, Lily?"

"Sometimes." Lily's smile held a touch of sadness. "I know Mother is trying to take some of the load of the three children off me, but I want Genevieve to grow up knowing *I'm* her mother." Lily shook her head. "I'm sorry, I sound very ungrateful."

"No, you don't. It is only natural for a mother to want to care for her own baby. It's nice to have some time off, but they are still your babies, and others don't have the same thing in mind for them that you do."

Lily heaved a big sigh and smiled. "Thanks. I've been feeling guilty 'cause I resent it every time Genevieve cries, and Mother beats me to her."

"I think Mother is trying to help you and has no idea that you feel this way. Having two active boys thrust on you with such a small baby can be a hardship. She thinks she is helping."

Tears welled in Lily's eyes. "I'm sorry, I feel like I'm being unthankful. And I'm not. I am so happy to be home with the only family I have ever had, I guess I am a bit jealous and holding on too tight. You are such a sharing bunch. I've never had much to share, so you're going to have to teach me how!"

Mary Lou laughed. "Oh, you'll learn. That's what a family is, a sharing bunch, in everything! If we didn't share the work, we'd drop from overload."

Lily rose, drained her glass, and set it on the table. "I'd best get going. Thanks." She patted Mary Lou's hand.

Mary Lou rose and they both stood and observed the children at play. Their squeals, giggles, and constant activity were a joy to watch.

Lily stepped out the door. "Wilmot, get hold of Baby Zack's hand. Time to go home."

Mary Lou stood by her house and watched Lily fade to about half size, then gathered her own two and went determinedly back to her garden.

sixteen

Tom and Zack waved goodbye to Allena and Mary Lou and rode off into the early mist of a hazy Texas morning on their way, at their mother's insistence, to check out the school building and see what repairs were needed, if any.

"It suited Anna Whitney, but I'm sure the new teacher will bring a lot of good ideas from her teaching experience in Virginia," had been their mother's comment.

So Zack had volunteered to consult with Miss Truesdale and supervise whatever repairs might be needed to enhance the school.

"Since you were schooled in the East, you will know better what we need here and don't forget your son will soon be a student there."

Zack had seen Eastern schools and agreed that much could be done to make better schools in Texas. Even state legislators were slowly realizing the growing interest Texans were expressing for the education of their children.

The school house was about five miles past the church. In comparison, the condition of the school house was noticeably lacking. Surrounding ranch families had expressed cooperation in their support of a better school. Those with children of school age had each promised to pay one dollar a month per pupil to the new teacher, Miss Ruthella Truesdale.

Tom and Zack trotted into the school yard and noticed a sidesaddled horse standing patiently ground-reined at one

144

corner. As they dismounted, Miss Truesdale appeared in the open doorway.

"Good morning, sirs." She smiled, looking very different from the elegant lady who had played the organ in church the day before. Today, she wore a dark skirt and a shirt waist with the long sleeves rolled halfway up her arm which she quickly brushed down and buttoned the cuffs.

Both men doffed their hats.

"Good morning, Miss Truesdale," Zack said.

Tom nodded. "Miss Truesdale."

"We are glad to find you here," Zack said. "We came to see what needs to be done to the school before it starts."

A wide smile spread across Miss Truesdale's face, revealing a row of very white, even teeth. "Oh, thank you. I just arrived myself and was standing in the middle of the classroom wondering where to start! Come in, gentlemen."

The clunk of the men's boot heels disturbed the quiet and the dust in a room that had obvious need of repairs.

"I wondered whom I would be responsible to, and where I could express my needs for my classroom," Miss Truesdale said.

Zack dropped his head, then lifted it with a grin. "I guess I'm sort of expected by the parents and my mother to see that you are situated. It will be my pleasure, ma'am."

Miss Truesdale nodded her head and swung around. "I see we do not have desks of any sort, just benches. Would it be at all possible to have long desks made along these two walls with benches for the older children so they can rest their arms to write properly? The benches are fine for the younger children at first." She moved to the opposite wall, turned and waved her arm across the large blackboard. "I'm pleased with this. It is a wonderful aid to teaching and children dearly love to write on it. It also gives them good practice since much of the time there is usually a dearth of writing paper."

Zack reached into his vest pocket and drew out a small notebook.

"And I wondered if there would be any objection if I allowed Miss Whitney to come in as she has strength and can teach special subjects. It will not cost the parents. We can both manage on the salary expressed." Miss Truesdale smiled. "You know, once a teacher, always a teacher."

Zack nodded and smiled. "The teaching of the children is your responsibility, Miss Truesdale. I'm sure Miss Whitney will be a great help to you. I was taught by her. In fact, my brothers and most of the folks who grew up here were taught by her. It was in deference to her that this schoolhouse was built by Will Shepard. She made a special trip to his ranch twice a week to teach him to read and write. Her failing health is the only reason we put out a call for a new teacher. I'm sure it would be hard for her to just sit by after all her faithful years of work."

Miss Truesdale nodded her head. "Thank you. She will also be teaching me because the school where I taught was much more structured, and I can see the variety and scope of work is much greater here. I accept the challenge."

Zack followed Miss Truesdale around the room, making jottings in his little book of her needs and comments. Before Tom and Zack left, Miss Whitney limped in, leaning heavily on her cane.

"My, my, look who's here," she said. A pleasant glow filled her face. She patted Zack's sleeve and turned to Miss Truesdale. "Here is my best pupil, Ruthella. No one ever studied harder than he did. He wanted to be a lawyer and despite all the obstacles, he did it." Miss Whitney patted Zack's arm again and smiled up into his face. "But it pleases me and I'm proud that after all that good education and opportunity you had in the East, you decided to come back home and use your knowledge for the benefit of Texas."

Miss Truesdale's eyebrows raised. She smiled and nodded to Zack.

Zack grinned. "Once a Texas boy, always a Texas boy, my mother says, and I proved her right."

They all laughed and Miss Whitney bobbed her head.

"How many children will be enrolling from your family?" Miss Truesdale asked.

"This year, a boy named Lars. He isn't one of our family, actually. Sort of adopted. But give us a few years, and you will have Wilmot, his brother, my son, and Tom's twins.

Miss Whitney nodded and looked up into Zack's face. "Oh, yes, and I haven't seen Darcy for some time. Is she still back East visiting her family?"

Zack's face became a mask. "Yes, ma'am." He didn't elaborate and turned to Tom. "Anything else you wanted to look at, repairs or something?"

Tom shook his head. He had a few questions, but sensed his brother's need to leave. They could be discussed elsewhere.

A slight twinge of Miss Truesdale's brows stated a question, then her face broadened with a smile and she made no comment. "I will be happy to meet all your children," she said cordially.

Tom and Zack mounted and left Miss Truesdale waving in the doorway where they found her.

At the road, Tom and Zack parted company, Zack off to Harness and Tom back to the ranch.

Tom and Tinder rode under the CIRCLE Z arch and stopped at the main ranch house.

His mother came out the door, stood and waited until he rode up beside her. She patted Tinder's neck and looked up. "Well? What did you think of Miss Truesdale?"

"She is a fine woman, and I think she will make an excellent teacher for my children," Tom said and grinned. "She sweet-talked Zack into some new desks and benches, and asked if Miss Whitney could help her in the classroom."

"Wonderful. My heart identifies with a woman being put out to pasture."

Tom frowned. "You—out to pasture?" He laughed. "I don't think I'll ever live to see that day."

Allena grinned. She hoped she would never see it either.

"Mary Lou here?" Tom asked.

"No, Lily just came home from there."

Tom swung Tinder. "That's where I better head for."

Allena nodded and watched her son trot off, then turned toward the sound of squealing children.

Tom rode to the corral first to check on Annie and her foals. She was thin. Smitty had brought an old mare work horse from the main ranch as a wet nurse. He should be able to wean those colts next month.

He laughed aloud as he watched Adam dart and dash everywhere and nowhere. Yesterday, he'd noticed that neither the colt nor the filly could walk under their mother's stomach anymore. Eve was noticeably smaller and trimmer. Pretty little thing, Tom thought. I'm surprised Nelson hasn't been out here with his easel painting those two.

He rode Tinder back to the barn, took off his saddle and

turned him out to pasture.

Walking toward the house, the tantalizing smell of food made him realize that he was hungry. When he opened the door, he found a frazzled wife with his daughter in tears. Tommy had just spilled a pitcher of milk and pulled Beth's hair.

Mary Lou looked up from the stove and pushed back a few wisps of hair that had lost their anchor and grinned at Tom. "Mama never told me there would be days like this. But then, all she had was one sweet little girl!"

Tom laughed and picked up his mischievous son. Beth put both arms around one of his legs and looked up expectantly.

Tom put both children in their high chairs, tied Tommy in his.

"Well—tell me about the new teacher. Was she at the school? Did she know you were coming? How does she like the schoolhouse?"

"Whoa! She was at the school. She did not know we were coming and she is a very lovely, gracious lady, and one who knows exactly what she wants. Zack has a list of what she needs and wants, plus she wants Miss Whitney to be able to help her when she is able."

"That's wonderful! I felt for that dear lady having to move out of the position she has held in this community for so long."

Mary Lou placed the last bowl on the table, sat down and bowed her head. Tommy took his cup, ducked his chin into his chest, and looked out of the tops of wide eyes.

Tom cupped his hand on his son's head. "Good boy," he said, bowed his own head and said grace.

seventeen

Tex watched from a bunkhouse window as Zack and Lily mounted and rode off toward the west. The only thing he knew in that direction within short riding distance was Zack's house.

Into his mind flashed a scene he'd watched from the barn of Zack riding in, dismounting, walking to meet Lily and Baby Zack; then, with Baby Zack between them, the three laughing as they rang the dinner bell. Tex's mind churned. *Zack and Lily. . . Darcy gone. . . Baby Zack needs a ma. . .*

Tex stared after the fading figures. After all, they are brother and sister-in-law. Maybe he just needs her advice about something at the house. Yet, Tex couldn't seem to convince himself of anything. The two figures grew smaller. He seethed inside with intense jealousy, an entirely new experience.

A horse and rider galloped from Zack's house. Tex squinted. *Looks like Pete.* His face spread with a wide grin. Bet he's up there workin'. Pete had told Tex he'd been helpin' Zack. As Tex watched, Pete met them, they talked, then all three rode to the house. Tex smiled, heaved a big sigh, and walked back into the horse barn and furiously cleaned stalls.

What is wrong with me? Tex jawed himself. Disturbing new feelings churned inside him. He had never felt this way before. Maybe it was time for him to move on. Not that he wanted to. He liked working for the Langdons. Good honest, family people, and he appreciated the fact that Tom treated him like a good friend. Of all the ranches he'd worked, the Circle Z topped them all.

"Tex? Are you in here?"

"Yes, ma'am." He walked through the barn to Mrs. Langdon.

"Has Zack said anything to you yet about building desks at the school?"

"Yes, ma'am."

"Would you have time to work at the school today? Miss Truesdale said she would like to have the desks made as soon as possible 'cause of the mess involved. She needs them finished so she can clean and set up the schoolroom to get ready for school next month. You finished with your work here?"

"Just about."

"Well, I'll have Hattie pack you a basket of food for dinner, enough for you, Miss Truesdale, and Miss Whitney, too. Tell the ladies a couple things will need to be heated. By the time you get your wagon loaded with the wood and tools, we'll have it ready." She turned and walked toward the house, then turned suddenly. "Oh, and Tex?"

"Yes, ma'am?"

"Why don't you take Lars? He's almost six. He's old enough to fetch for you. Besides, I think he needs to become acquainted with his new teacher. Maybe if he gets to know her, he might be a little more eager to go to school. This morning he told me he's not going, 'cause he's going to be a cowboy, just like you." Allena couldn't contain her smile.

Tex ducked his head but it didn't conceal his satisfied

grin. "Well, ma'am, we'll have to see 'bout that!"

Within an hour, Tex had his chores done, the wagon loaded with wood, and tools waiting in front of the house.

The door bounced open, out flew Lars, his face beaming. He climbed on the wagon hub and scrambled onto the seat beside Tex. "Lily's mama said I'm going to be your fetch boy!"

Tex laughed. "That's right. Do you promise to work real hard and do what I tell ya?" Tex yanked Lars' cowboy hat down over his eyes.

"Yep." Lars laughed and righted his hat.

Allena and Hattie came out, each with a basket, and Tex put the baskets in a space he had saved for them.

"Thank ya, ma'am." Tex nodded and swung the team toward the CIRCLE Z arch. In what seemed like no time at all, they bumped across the school yard. Tex leaped from his seat.

Lars prepared to jump like Tex, changed his mind, scrambled down over the wheel and stood at Tex's side. He glanced up at Tex who removed his hat when the lady came out of the schoolhouse door.

"Take off your hat, boy, in the presence of a lady," Tex said softly.

Lars shot a quick look at Tex, removed his hat, held it in his hand in front of him like Tex, stood up straight beside him and watched the lady come out the door and walk toward them.

"Good afternoon, gentlemen. You must be Tex. Mr. Zack Langdon stopped by this morning on his way to Harness and told me you might be able to come today." She looked down at Lars and smiled. "And who is this young man?"

"This is Lars Zigwald, and he will be your pupil when school starts next month."

"Oh, so you are the boy from the Langdons who will be starting school this year?"

"No, ma'am. I'm going to be a cowboy like Tex." He looked up at his idol.

Tex frowned down at Lars, shifted his feet and looked up in apology to Miss Truesdale. "Yes, he is, ma'am. He don't quite understand 'bout school yet."

Miss Truesdale smiled and nodded. "I see." She turned and walked back toward the school. "Come in, gentlemen, and I'll show you what needs to be done."

After dinner, halfway through the afternoon, the wood had been sawed to fit, and Tex, with Lars fetchin', had the big desk built on the long wall.

Miss Truesdale came in periodically and gave forth constant praise. She watched Lars for a while, then suddenly asked, "Lars, don't you think if you are going to be a cowboy like Tex and have to build barns and maybe schoolhouses, you had better learn your numbers so you can count and measure like him?"

Lars shot a quick glance at Tex. "Did you go to school when you were like me, Tex?"

Tex shot a desperate glance at Miss Truesdale, who gave him a reassuring nod.

Miss Truesdale laid her hand on the top of Lars' head. "Now Tex must have had schooling of some kind to learn his numbers like he knows them, wouldn't he, Lars?"

Lars looked from Miss Truesdale to Tex and thought for a minute. "Did some teacher learn you your numbers?" he asked Tex.

Miss Truesdale cupped Lars' chin in her hand and turned

his face up to her. "Now think, Lars. Somebody had to teach him." She looked up and smiled at Tex. "Didn't they, Tex?"

"Yes, ma'am. Why—uh—somebody did teach me my numbers." He looked down into Lars' face. "And somebody's got to teach you yours."

Lars questioning eyes focused on Miss Truesdale's teacher-face. "Did somebody teach you your numbers, ma'am?"

Very seriously, Miss Truesdale nodded her head. "Aboslutely! I learned them in school."

"If I come to school, will you teach me numbers?"

Miss Truesdale nodded her head decisively. "Yes, Lars, I certainly will."

Tex's gaze spoke his thanks. "I'll see what Tom and Miz Langdon have for me tomorrow. When I get a chance, Lars and I will be back to build the rest."

Lars stood straight. "Yes ma'm. We'll come."

Tex unloaded most of the wood from the wagon and put it inside the school to keep dry.

"I am so pleased, gentlemen. I can see we are going to be finished in plenty of time before the first day at school. I thank you for your good work."

"'Tis a pleasure, ma'am. It won't take too long to finish the small wall. Since I have the measures, I can finish the benches in my spare time at the ranch." Tex hoisted Lars onto his seat.

Miss Truesdale stood in the door and waved as they drove off.

Anna Whitney walked around the schoolhouse and watched them go. "That cowboy is a good young man, but what you need is a learned gentleman," she said and glanced up at Ruthella.

Ruthella's mouth dropped open, then spread into a smile. "Anna Whitney! Do I sense a little matchmaking?"

"I'm just saying he's a very nice young man for a cow-boy, but not for you. I had a nice talk with Allena Langdon the other day when she stopped by the day you went to town. I asked her about Zack's wife, and she told me that Darcy will not live in Texas and has had her lawyer father arrange a quiet divorce."

Ruthella's mouth flew open. "Zack is a divorced man?"

"Yes, but it isn't his fault. I've known Zack Langdon all his life. He was the best student I ever had, a very intelli-gent young man. I must admit I had a hard time liking Darcy and still don't understand what he saw or how the Langdon family put up with her. She was too uppity and seldom spoke to people here. She showed me with her snooty ways that she thought us beneath her. They had one little boy who is crippled in one leg. When Baby Zack was born, Darcy was so upset about that she didn't want anything to do with him. If you want to hear my say, I think he's better off without her. She was the wrong wife for such a fine man as Zack Langdon."

Miss Truesdale didn't say a word, but her brows drew together in thought.

"And Zack's more your level, Ruthella, and the best catch for you around here."

Ruthella laughed and shook her head. "Anna Whitney! You are an old cupid. I'm not even thinking of getting married, especially to a divorced man. I am a school teacher. I have to be an upstanding example to my stu-dents."

Anna shook her head. "I thought like you once. I'm

sorry I didn't accept the nice young man who loved me. If I had, I wouldn't now be old and alone and could be enjoying the blessing of my children in my old age." Anna rose and thumped after her cane to the door and turned. "Well, my dear, you think about it. My opportunity to marry a good, loving man came only once,. My refusal of his loving offer was the biggest mistake of my life." Anna thumped out.

Ruthella sat down on a bench. Her mind pictured the tall and handsome dark-haired man who had sat in church on the end of the bench beside her. Zack had manners, and Ruthella liked a well-mannered man. When she had come from the organ, he had risen, waited until she was seated, then sat down beside her.

She remembered his neat, trim appearance when he had stopped on his way to town yesterday to tell her Tex would be doing the building. She ducked her head and smiled, remembering her heart had beat a little faster in his presence.

She gasped an intake of breath. *Ruthella Truesdale!* She chastised herself within. *Come to your senses.* She stood and hurried across the floor and out the schoolhouse door, banging it behind her. *God, forgive me for indulging in such foolish thinking.*

She slowed as she neared the little cabin behind the schoolhouse. Anna's pathetic, wistful confession pierced her heart. *I could be like her some day.* Something shriveled inside her. *No! No!* her heart protested. She walked into the cabin and straight to her room to hide her welling tears.

eighteen

The whole family gathered for supper.

"Emily Shepard and I have been talking about having a big harvest barbeque here at the Circle Z," Allena announced as they sat around the table enjoying Hattie's mincemeat pie and coffee.

Tom nodded. "Sounds like a good idea to me. It's been a good year. The ranchers have worked hard. We need to gather in fellowship and thanks for God's bounty."

Family discussion bounced back and forth across the supper table and finally settled for the first Saturday in October.

Zack cleared his throat. "There is some business the family needs to discuss about the ranch. Can we go into the office for a short meeting?"

Zack seated his mother in Father Zack's big leather chair and faced his brothers. "Mother and I have been talking about Lily. We feel that since she was Doug's wife, and Genevieve is Doug's child, some inheritance should be arranged. Mother suggested we give Doug's share of the ranch to Genevieve, and with Tex and Lily contemplating marriage, we thought to give them an interest in the land if Tex works it, with the stipulation that at Tex and Lily's deaths, the land reverts back to Langdon property and will belong exclusively to Genevieve."

A silence of churning minds and a short discussion brought all family members into agreement. They returned

157

to the dining room table, and Tom went out to the barn to get Tex.

When they returned, Zack laid the offer on the table.

Lily stared first at Zack, then Allena, stunned.

"Well, Tex," Tom grinned. "You always said you wanted your own spread."

Both Tex and Lily were speechless.

After more discussion, Zack said, "Then I'll draw up the papers, and after they are signed and presented to the judge and the clerk, it will be done."

Lily glanced around the family with tear-filled eyes. "God bless you. You're more family than I ever hoped for. Thank you." Her tears allowed no more words. She gazed at Tex.

His eyes were shining and moved from Zack to Allena to Nelson and finally rested on Tom. In a choked voice, he said, "Thank you good people. I'll work hard to help you make the Circle Z the best ranch in Texas."

Everyone laughed.

Zack scanned the faces at the table. "Then all is in agreement. I'll see to it on Monday."

The following week, Hattie and Lily volunteered to stay home and care for all the children while Allena and Mary Lou took the day to visit surrounding ranches. They found everyone enthusiastic and delighted. Allena told Zack to stop at the school and invite Miss Truesdale and Anna, also to check and see if Dr. Mike could make it, or leave a note telling him about it if he wasn't there.

Two days before the barbeque found Mary Lou busy at her cookstove. Lily had come early in the morning and took Tommy and Beth to the main house to play. As she watched them toddle toward the main ranch, Mary Lou stretched, relaxed in the released free feeling without them—free to work.

She laid her hand on the stove and held it there until she counted to twenty. The warmth told her practiced hand the oven was ready so she slid three raised loaves of bread inside to bake. A big pot of beef stew for supper simmered on the top.

She walked to the new chicken coop Tom had built between the house and her vegetable garden, close enough for her to care for her chickens, but also far enough to release them into the vegetable garden to help Mary Lou keep ahead of the bugs. She smiled. Everything on a ranch has to earn its keep. She caught three old hens, chopped off their heads, removed the entrails, and kept the liver, heart, and gizzard to make giblets in the gravy, then hung the chickens by their feet on the high line to drain. She'd wash and pluck them later and put them into a stew pot.

She worked steadily all day. By the middle of the afternoon, she had made pie shells for pumpkin pies. She had two pumpkins perched outside the kitchen door next to the chairs where she and Tom sat. Hopefully, they could get the pumpkin all ready to put in the pie shells to bake first thing in the morning. Spread everywhere were freshly baked cookies and bread, two large pans of chicken pie awaiting tender biscuit dough tops, and their allotted time in the oven. She even had enough buttermilk from her freshly made butter to make cottage cheese.

About three in the afternoon, she glanced around the kitchen, then at the clock and smiled. My, how much she had accomplished without the twins! She washed her face, put on a clean apron, smoothed her hair, and began her walk down to the main ranch house to get her children.

From afar, she watched Lily cross from the house to the barn. The children must be asleep. She waved.

Lily paused, waved at Mary Lou, then proceeded to the barn for Lars. Poor Tex. She wondered how he worked with that boy under his feet most of the time. Tex was a good, patient man. He would make a great father. She could hear voices across the stalls.

As they came into view, Lars stood beside Tex, barely giving him room to breathe. "Lars! Step back and give Tex room to work."

Tex turned and greeted her with a warm, welcoming smile.

"Don't you get a little weary of Lars tagging you all the time?"

Tex shook his head and grinned. "No. He's good company, and learns fast. A cowboy's life is a lonely life. . ." He glanced into Lily's eyes.

The longing she saw in his eyes took her by surprise. She tried to divert her eyes but they refused to move. Was that tenderness she saw in his face? Or—could it be— love?

Tex broke their gaze and quickly busied himself cinching the saddle, picked Lars up and swung him onto the horse's back. "Lars and I were going to take a riding lesson. Want me to saddle you up a horse so's you can ride with us?"

"Just a minute," she said, "I'll see if they can spare me. We have a houseful of children." Had Lily seen a wisp of pleading in his gaze or was she misreading him because she wanted it that way? She turned and hustled across the yard and disappeared through the ranch door. Almost as fast as she went in, she reappeared and hurried back to the barn.

"Mother says I need a rest and to take a ride with you and Lars, and it will give you a rest as well. She said you've been working very hard lately."

Tex saddled another horse, handed the reins to Lily, mounted his own, grabbed the reins of Lars' horse and put him between them.

They rode to the chatter of Lars asking questions about everything they passed, he saw or thought. All of a sudden, he quieted. Both Lily and Tex looked at him to see if something was wrong. Their eyes met across the top of the boy's head.

Lars looked first at Tex, then at Lily. "Lily, why don't you marry Tex so he can be my Pa?"

Silence reverberated the air.

After a long moment, Lily laughed. "Lars, I think it's time for you to stop talking and listen. You cannot talk all the time. It's polite to allow others to speak as well as you."

Tex pulled his and Lars horse to a halt.

Lily rode ahead, stopped suddenly, turned and was swallowed by Tex's questioning gaze.

Tex laughed and ducked his head. "Well, fella," he said and turned his eyes to Lily. "That ain't the way it's done, Lars. First, you have to find out if the girl you want to marry wants to marry you.

"Sure she does!" Lars answered.

Tex turned stern eyes at Lars. "Be quiet, boy." He glanced at Lily and his face reddened.

Time hung awaiting.

"Well, Lars," Lily began hesitantly, "a girl first has to know whether a man is in love with her or not."

Lars looked at Lily. "Are you in love with Tex, Lily?"

"Lars!" Lily ducked her head, then raised up laughing, two very red spots flooding her cheeks.

Tex moved his mount up beside Lily. "I'd like to know the answer to that myself."

The tender look in his eyes warmed Lily's heart. "What would you do, Tex, if I said 'yes?'" She drank in the love he poured from his eyes. "Do you realize if you married me you would not only get Lars, but Wilmot and Genevieve as well?"

Tex, beaming, slipped from his horse, hauled Lars to the ground, walked over to Lily and held up his arms.

Lily slid off the horse into them. Tex gazed at her a moment, then pressed his hungry lips over hers. "I'll take anything if I can have you for my wife."

Lily closed her eyes and tasted the sweetness of his mouth on hers and felt his heart pounding his love. For the first time in her life she felt comfortable in a man's arms. This was where she belonged. His arms encircling her were more wonderful than she had ever dreamed.

Lars stared up at them. His little brows bent into a frown as they kissed. Suddenly, his eyes brightened and his mouth stretched into a wide grin. "Does that mean you are married, and Tex is my Pa?"

Tex smiled at Lily, and they turned to the boy. "Almost!"

Tex swung Lars up on his horse, grabbed the lines of the other two, put his arm around Lily and they walked back to the barn.

nineteen

Zack turned into the school yard on his way to Harness.

Suddenly the cabin door opened and Miss Truesdale came through and walked toward Zack. She was dressed in a soft blue dress that made her look delicate and fragile.

Zack halted, dismounted, waved his hand and smiled in greeting. "Good morning, Miss Truesdale, you are just the one I want to see."

"Oh?"

Zack had to admit it. She was a pretty woman. His heart remembered another pretty woman. His mind shut the door. It was over and the sooner he forgot her, the better. "I'm here to invite you and Miss Whitney to the barbecue at our house this coming Saturday. We are celebrating God's good harvest, and ranchers and neighbors all round these parts will be coming." He nodded at Miss Truesdale. "This will be a nice way for you to meet many of your pupils and their families. I'm sure they are curious about you."

"Probably wondering whether they will get another cranky, old teacher," Anna said from the doorway.

Zack laughed. "Miss Whitney, if you are talking about yourself, be careful, I just might agree with you." He turned to Ruthella. "Talk about strict! If we dared wiggle our ears crooked, she boxed them."

"Zachary Langdon! You come here this minute and let me wash out your mouth with soap for telling a lie!"

163

They laughed.

Miss Truesdale looked at Anna. "Are you up to a day-long affair?"

"I can sit there just as well as here, except I will have the pleasure of talking to many I haven't seen for a while." Miss Whitney looked with pleasure at Zack. "Thank your good mother for thinking of us."

"Good. I will come with the buggy Saturday at ten." Zack gazed fondly at the ladies. He lingered a couple moments longer to bask in the glow of Miss Truesdale's brown eyes. He quickly mounted and waved. "My mother will be delighted. Good day, ladies." Zack turned Victor's head toward Harness and rode off.

The day of the barbecue dawned warm and sunny. A perfect day. The men busied themselves setting up saw horses, boards, and benches. In a clear spot at the end of the barn closest to the house, Jess and several of the cowboys already had the steer strung up on the spit. The acrid odor of the animal's seared flesh permeated the air.

Wagons, horses, buggies of neighbors, including the Shepards, pulled into the space at the end of the barn. Each family carried armfulls of food with tempting aromas to a long row of sawhorse tables and deposited their donations to the feast. A festive mood took hold with back-slapping, joshing comradery among the men, organizing chatter among the women, and wide-eyed excitement of the children playing nonsense games.

Crops, cows, steer, hunting, windmills, the impact of the railroads were thrashed over, argued over, and laughed over. Yet a spirit of optimism pervaded the conversations, generated by everyone's fierce love of Texas.

Come late afternoon, one by one the neighbors reboarded

their wagons, pulled out with hearty goodbyes, and wended their ways toward home. Some had a good hour's ride compounded with cranky, exhausted children who had run themselves ragged, still exhilarated by an excess of play-mates. It had been a joyous day.

Tom suggested that Mary Lou, Zack, and Miss Truesdale ride up and see Zack's house before he took her home. Fortunately, Allena had an old English side saddle that she dusted off for the teacher.

The sun had traveled three-quarters of its daily trip and hung as a huge orange ball in the west when the foursome rode off.

They rode four abreast when possible, but at one part of the trail, they had to break into two's. Zack and Tom rode ahead and Ruthella, who insisted Mary Lou call her by her given name, dropped slightly behind.

"The Circle Z is a magnificent ranch," Ruthella commented.

Mary Lou scanned the familiar landscape. "Yes, it is."

"I never realized the wide openness of the West. Back in Virginia, we have open land, but I guess it is because there are more trees, or something. It seems so big here."

Mary Lou laughed. "It *is* big here. At my home in Kansas, I grew up in wide, open spaces."

Ruthella nodded slowly.

When they reached Zack's house, the men dismounted and came back to escort the ladies.

Mary Lou and Tom walked behind Zack who held Ruthella's arm. It was obvious to Mary Lou that she was impressed with the beauty of the house, and like any woman, probably envisisoned the curtains up and imaginary furniture all set in place.

Pounding of hooves turned their attention to a rider galloping pell-mell spewing a dust trail behind him.

"Tom! Mary Lou! Come back. Dr. Mike says Tommy broke his leg!" he called.

Tom and Mary Lou were on their horses by the time the rider reached them. The three swung around and raced back to the ranch.

Zack and Ruthella said, "Oh, we must be going, too."

Zack reached out his hand and stopped her. "Now that we are here, it won't hurt to take a few minutes to see the house. There is nothing we can do for Tommy. I'm sure he has enough nursemaids."

Ruthella gazed self-consciously around her, her discomfort magnified by the intense gaze of the man in front of her.

"Miss Truesdale, do you believe that sometimes God arranges things for us when we don't seem to manage for ourselves?"

"What? Why—why—I don't know quite what you mean, Mr. Langdon."

Zack smiled and rubbed his chin. "Well, I've been trying to find a moment alone with you all day to talk to you."

"Mr. Langdon!" Ruthella's heart behaved curiously.

"Miss Truesdale, I would like permission to visit you, if I may." Ruthella looked up into his face horrified. "But—you're—a—"

"Divorced man? I can understand why you would be concerned, Miss Truesdale. But Miss Whitney told me she thought you and I were very well suited to one another."

"Anna! Why—how could she say such a thing?"

Zack reached for Ruthella's hand. He felt her tug it

away slightly, but held on. "For a lawyer, who should know how to discuss difficult situations, I've botched this badly. Forgive me, Ruthel—forgive me, Miss Truesdale. What I am trying to ask you is will you allow me the privilege of coming to see you? We can be in the presence of Miss Whitney, if you wish. I know you are used to the different amenities and ways of the East. Unfortunately, here in the West, we don't have time nor the means to execute all the niceties of Virginia."

Ruthella relaxed her hand. She stood still and darted her eyes back and forth between the broad shoulder and the brown eyes of the man in front of her, acutely aware of the warm, strong hand that held hers. Finally she anchored her gaze on his eyes. They seemed to search her soul. "Mr. Langdon, I am fully aware of my inadequacies in this big land of Texas. But I know my ways are not the only ways. When I see the tender respect and caring your family and your neighbors have for each other—and others—I—uh—will be very pleased with your company. You may come visit whenever you choose."

Zack bent, kissed the back of Ruthella's hand and released it. "Thank you." Gentlemanly, he cupped her elbow and guided her into the four bare walls of the dining room. They strolled through the other rooms. "The stairway has not yet been built, but one of the cowboys helping to build the house came from Virginia and says he knows how they build those famous stairways in Virginia. Virginia is famous for its magnificent stairways. I'd appreciate it if you would talk to him so it will be built the way you want—the way you think right."

As they walked to their horses, Zack smothered an inclination to circle his hands around Ruthella's tiny waist and lift her into her saddle, but thought the better of it, bent and cupped his hands for her foot and assisted her onto the saddle.

They trotted leisurely back to the ranch. Zack was newly aware of a loving Hand on their lives who planted in his heart the hope that Ruthella would—somehow—sometime—become his wife. He was sure of one thing. The love he had for her, he had never felt toward Darcy. He sensed her love for him, but she was afraid of it. And, this time he'd take his time. An illuminating thought surfaced. He had never asked Darcy to marry him! It had been assumed.

They rode into the ranch yard. The last of the visiting wagons had left. Tommy's leg was strapped to a piece of wood he kept trying to take off. Finally, he sat staring at his leg with his thumb in his mouth which he removed every so often to allow his teary babble to escape.

Hattie shoed Mary Lou away from the food. "Don't fuss with this. Someone will bring it up to the house tomorrow morning."

"Better yet," Allena interrupted, "just plan to eat here every meal so we can use up this cooked food."

"Sounds good to me," Mary Lou said. "Thank you, Mother."

Tex saddled up one of the buggies for Tom to take his family home. Tom patted him on the shoulder. "Thanks, Tex, see you in the morning. You can help me fight with Adam and Eve. Time to separate them from their mother."

Tex nodded.

Tom gave a slap with the reins.

Tommy whimpered through his thumb and Beth's head wobbled in sleep on the way home. Both Tom and Mary

Lou undressed them and unwashed, rolled them into bed both sound asleep.

It had been a memorable day.

Tom went out to the barn to do chores and check the animals.

Mary Lou pumped some cold water and made vinegar-ginger tea.

If she hadn't been so tired, she would have walked to the barn. Instead, she sat down on one of the chairs in the front of their house and watched the sinking sun cling tenaciously to the edge of the horizon.

She thought of the glow on Ruthella's face when she and Zack came back from his house. And did she imagine a spring in Zack's step as he assisted Ruthella and Miss Whitney into the buggy when he took them home? Mary Lou laughed. Looked like she might have a real sister-in-law yet!

Allena had told her of Lily and Tex. *Brave man that Tex! He's not only marrying Lily, he's marrying a whole family!*

Thank You, dear God. Why is it we don't fully realize that our best interest is in Your precious will? You want to give Your children a thousand times more than they want to receive.

An old familiar warmth washed over Mary Lou. She looked up and smiled. Mama? "I'm still praying for Pa to accept the Lord Jesus as his Savior, Mama. God never gives up on anyone and neither will I," Mary Lou whispered softly.

Tom emerged from the barn and walked through the shadowy twilight.

Mary Lou slid out of her reverie, suddenly aware of the

tears on her lashes and cheeks. She glanced up at Tom standing in front of her and smiled. His brows squinted a question.

"Looked like you were in another world, my dear. Welcome back." He bent over and squinted into her eyes. "It is too dark for me to see but was that your Kansas or your Mama look?"

Mary Lou stood up, slipped her arms around her husband and gazed into those clear, blue pools she fell into when she met him. She slowly shook her head. "It was neither this time." Mary Lou smiled. "It was my Texas look."

Tom's brows raised, then a knowing grin creased his tanned face. "Welcome home, Mrs. Langdon."

A Letter To Our Readers

Dear Reader:

In order that we might better contribute to your reading enjoyment, we would appreciate your taking a few minutes to respond to the following questions. When completed, please return to the following:

Rebecca Germany, Editor
Heartsong Presents
P.O. Box 719
Uhrichsville, Ohio 44683

1. Did you enjoy reading *Pioneer Legacy*?
   ❏ Very much. I would like to see more books
      by this author!
   ❏ Moderately
      I would have enjoyed it more if _____

   _____

2. Are you a member of *Heartsong Presents*? Yes   No
   If no, where did you purchase this book? _____

   _____

3. What influenced your decision to purchase this
   book? (Check those that apply.)

      ❏ Cover   ❏ Back cover copy

      ❏ Title   ❏ Friends

      ❏ Publicity   ❏ Other _____

4. On a scale from 1 (poor) to 10 (superior), please rate the following elements.

___Heroine   ___Plot

___Hero   ___Inspirational theme

___Setting   ___Secondary characters

5. What settings would you like to see covered in *Heartsong Presents* books?

_____

_____

6. What are some inspirational themes you would like to see treated in future books?_____

_____

_____

7. Would you be interested in reading other *Heartsong Presents* titles?   ❑ Yes   ❑ No

8. Please check your age range:
❑ Under 18   ❑ 18-24   ❑ 25-34
❑ 35-45   ❑ 46-55   ❑ Over 55

9. How many hours per week do you read? _____

Name _____

Occupation _____

Address _____

City _____ State _____ Zip _____

Norene Morris

Historical Trilogy

___***Cottonwood Dreams***—The pioneer town of Venture, Kansas was all Mary Lou had ever known. One day changed everything. Mary Lou longed to be a rancher's wife. Was it time to give up her dream? HP12 $2.95

___***Rainbow Harvest***—Newly married Mary Lou and Tom leave her frontier home in Kansas for Tom's ranch in Texas. Mary Lou and Tom have seen God work miracles in their own lives. Now they are praying that God will bring a similar harvest in the lives of those they love. HP39 $2.95

___***Pioneer Legacy***—Traveling from Texas to Kansas in the late 1800s, Mary Lou and Tom Langdon, along with their twins, have many trying experiences. As her old home looms nearer, Mary Lou wonders how she and her family will be received. HP107 $2.95

...... Presents ......

Heartsong Presents
Love Stories Are Rated G!

That's for godly, gratifying, and of course, great! If you love a thrilling love story, but don't appreciate the sordidness of popular paperback romances, **Heartsong Presents** is for you. In fact, **Heartsong Presents** is the *only inspirational romance book club*, the only one featuring love stories where Christian faith is the primary ingredient in a marriage relationship.

Sign up today to receive your first set of four, never before published Christian romances. Send no money now; you will receive a bill with the first shipment. You may cancel at any time without obligation, and if you aren't completely satisfied with any selection, you may return the books for an immediate refund!

Imagine. . .four new romances every month—two historical, two contemporary—with men and women like you who long to meet the one God has chosen as the love of their lives. . .all for the low price of $9.97 postpaid.

To join, simply complete the coupon below and mail to the address provided. **Heartsong Presents** romances are rated G for another reason: They'll arrive *Godspeed!*